T0128044

ORGASMIC

ORGASMIC

EROTICA FOR WOMEN

EDITED BY
RACHEL KRAMER BUSSEL

Published in the United States.
Cleis Press Inc., 221 River Street, 9th Floor, Hoboken, NJ 07030

Printed in the United States.
Cover design: Scott Idleman
Cover photograph: Hans Neleman/Getty Images
Text design: Frank Wiedemann
Cleis logo art: Juana Alicia
First Edition.
10 9 8 7 6 5 4 3 2 1

ISBN: 978-1-57344-402-6

Contents

INTRODUCTION: LET ME COUNT THE WAYS...

O*rgasm:* like *sex,* it's one word that means many different things to many different people. For many women, it's the center of their sexual life, a daily occurrence; something to look forward to, experiment with. For some, it means a gushing rush of pleasure; for others, it's a little wave they delight in cresting.

Every woman who orgasms may describe it differently.

Yet there are many women, myself included, who find orgasm not so easy to achieve much of the time (yes, it's true—I love sex, and get turned on, but coming is a bit more complex for me). In "Hurdles," Rowan Elizabeth writes of such a character: "I can't win this. And it's my hang-up, too. I feel like there's something I'm just not doing right. Maybe if I tighten my legs a little more or squeeze my eyes shut harder, then we'd get there together."

Merriam-Webster's Dictionary defines orgasm as "intense or paroxysmal excitement; especially: an explosive discharge of neuromuscular tensions at the height of sexual arousal that is usually accompanied by the ejaculation of semen in the male and by vaginal contractions in the female." It comes from the Latin and Greek (*orgasmus/orgasmos*), from *organ* "to grow ripe, be lustful." I like that description, though what it leaves out is that for women, orgasm can stretch beyond the boundaries of ejaculation, can continue on and on, can be drawn out for as long as the woman (or her partner) wants to indulge in the experience.

In Lolita Lopez's perfectly kinky story, "The Chair," sex toys and submission go hand in hand with orgasm for the protagonist. "Lily's orgasms changed from separate events to one long and unending oscillation of bliss." Her "punishment" at the hands of Cal is one she's very, very happy to absorb.

There are countless articles and books telling you how to have a bigger, better orgasm. I don't want to add to the clamor of the voices saying, *You must orgasm now.* Instead, I want *Orgasmic* to be a fictional showcase of some of the reasons, methods and delights women bring to their orgasms. I want these red-hot stories to help get you warmed up, primed, aroused. I want them to make you squirm with desire, identification, curiosity. I want you to read these stories aloud to a lover...or someone you wish were your lover.

I did my best to capture an array of big (and little) Os, moments where the world feels like it's exploding in your body, orgasms that rock more than just your world. These stories capture the ferocity, intensity and power of women's orgasms, however they're achieved. I couldn't include every way women come in this book, or it would be much longer than it is now, but I wanted to include a varied look at what gets women off, which means it's not always a man or another woman, or even a machine that does the trick. Vanessa Vaughn taps into a classic route with "Taking the Reins":

> As I straddle the seat and slowly lower myself down, I feel a familiar tingle of excitement deep inside. I can sense the monstrous size of the body between my thighs, the large chest expanding and contracting broadly with each breath. The smell of fresh, conditioned leather smothers my senses—well, that, and also the slight musky tinge of sweat. It is a raw smell mixed with rich, dark dirt.

Speaking of orgasm how-tos, in "The Big O" by Donna George Storey, she both skewers the omnipresent women's magazine sex advice and adds a saucy twist as her protagonist puts into practice "The Sexercise Prescription: A Stronger Secret You in Six Weeks."

The women in *Orgasmic* climax from tantric sex, role-playing, piercing, G-spot play, sex toys and even chemistry—the scientific kind. They delight in food, God and handymen. They create their own objects of pleasure; they spy, tease, obey, command, argue, submit. Some are shy about their orgasms and some are bold as can be.

They come, and come and come again, and they do it in some of the hottest, most creative ways you can think of. Visit me at orgasmicbook.wordpress.com if you just can't get enough... orgasms, that is.

Rachel Kramer Bussel
New York City

THE WAITING GAME

Elizabeth Coldwell

It starts with a simple game of cards, just another way of passing the time on this washout of a holiday. When Danny and I booked the cottage, intending to get away from the pressures of work for a week, we had visions of long walks along the beach and dinner in cozy country pubs. Instead, we've had three days of the worst weather in living memory. It's too wet to go anywhere or see anything; all we've done is lounge in front of the fire, working our way through the shelf of battered old paperbacks the owners have thoughtfully left in the living room. And then Danny, searching a drawer in the hope of finding a box of matches and sparing himself a dash out in the rain to the local shop, finds the cards.

I half expect him to suggest we play strip poker, but he's never been that predictable and besides, neither of us really knows the rules. Looking for a game that is slightly more intellectually stimulating than Snap, we settle on Cheat. As we work our way steadily through a bottle of chardonnay and a big bag of tortilla chips, we're soon howling with laughter and calling each other a cheat at every opportunity. Danny suggests that to make things more interesting, if either of us is caught declaring a card he or she hasn't got or makes an incorrect challenge, then that player should pay a forfeit. I ask him what he has in mind and he just smiles. I don't worry about it too much; I can usually tell when he's bluffing because he's no good at keeping his expression neutral. If we were playing strip poker, I'd have him down to his boxers by now.

So when Danny announces that he's got an ace, I simply have to challenge him: three have already come out, and the remaining one is in my hand, ready to be played. "Cheat!" I yell, and he turns the card over. To my incredulity, I'm looking at the ace of spades.

"That can't be possible," I say. "There have to be five aces in the pack."

Danny snorts derisively. "You're just a bad loser, Jade. Looks like you're going to have to pay that forfeit."

I could argue, but I'm already beginning to wonder whether I actually imagined the ace I thought I was holding. "Okay, what do you want me to do?"

Even before he tells me, I'm fairly sure it's going to be something sexual and more than likely something humiliating. Danny isn't cruel, but he does like to try to convince me he's the boss in our relationship. And I'll admit that sometimes I would like him to take control, if only he knew it; there's a dirty little part of me that gets unaccountably excited at the thought of my laid-back husband suddenly asserting his dominance over me. Maybe he'll order me to strip off and run around outside, naked in the cold October rain. Or maybe he'll whip out his cock and demand a blow job.

Yes, it'll be the blow job. I'm already preparing to get down on my knees in front of him when his reply stops me in my tracks. "It's more what I don't want you to do," he says. "Your forfeit is that you aren't going to be allowed to come until I give you permission."

So it *is* a control game. And I think I know why he's chosen this particular one.

I've never been one of those women who want—or need— orgasm after orgasm. Indeed, I've found the more frequently I come, the weaker, less enjoyable and harder to achieve those climaxes become. Whereas if I haven't come for a few days, the release is so strong, so all consuming that it leaves me spent and thoroughly satisfied. I once mentioned this to Danny, early on in our relationship, and while it's usually meant that he's never tried to bring me to a second orgasm in a night, knowing I'm completely happy with the first, now he's using that information to take our sex play to an entirely different level.

"And are you going to give me any idea how long I might have to wait?" I ask.

He shakes his head, an evil smile crossing his handsome features. "It might be before the end of the holiday—then again, it might not. All I will say is that by the time I do let you come, you'll be wanting it more than you ever have."

I think that's the end of it for the time being, but then he adds, "Now, I want you to go into the bedroom and get that little vibrator of yours. I know you've brought it with you, so don't pretend you don't know what I'm talking about. Bring it back here, there's a good girl."

The emphasis he places on the words "good girl" makes me shiver, and I wonder how long Danny has actually been thinking about making something like this happen.

My vibrator is tucked in the side pocket of my suitcase, wrapped in an innocent-looking pink silk scarf. It's small but powerful and has never let me down—which might not be a good thing, given the rule Danny has just outlined. I drop a couple of batteries into the chamber and return to the living room, where Danny has spread a towel on the sofa cushions. He's also brought a bottle of olive oil from the kitchen. Extra-virgin, I notice, looking at the viscous greenish liquid, and I realize my mind is trying to seek any diversion from what might be about to happen.

"I'm sure you've already guessed what I want you to do," he says. "Slip your knickers off, make yourself comfortable and use the vibrator on yourself. I brought you a little something for lubrication, just in case you need it."

He hands me the bottle with a little smirk. I'm squirming inside, but the way he's treating me, with a hint of arrogance and condescension so lacking in his usual personality, is turning me on like no one's business.

Danny sits in the rocking chair by the fireplace to watch. He's refilled his wineglass and looks as though he's settling in to enjoy the show. I'm wearing my favorite pair of pajama bottoms, navy blue with pink and white polka dots. They might be ideal for lounging around the house, but I know I'm going to have to take them off as well as my knickers.

My husband's eyes never leave me as I shimmy out of my clothing. It's warm in the cottage but my skin is suddenly bristling with goose bumps as I stand before him, naked from the waist down. He doesn't say a word, but I know his gaze is fixed squarely on the triangle of hair between my legs, freshly waxed for our holiday. Though he's trying his best to remain impassive, the distinct bulge forming at the front of his jogging bottoms can't help but give his real feelings away.

The bottle of oil is heavy in my hand as I unscrew the top. I feel strangely self-conscious as I lie back on the towel and spread my legs, even though Danny has seen me half-undressed so many times before. The difference is I'm not usually being required to exhibit myself for him, nor to drizzle oil along my hairless pussy lips till I can feel it trickling down over my tight little rosebud. This extra lubrication won't really be necessary, but it makes what I'm being asked to do all the ruder. Danny shifts in his seat as I switch on the vibrator, its buzzing surprisingly loud; he's no longer able to resist the temptation to cup and stroke his cock as he watches.

Knowing he's getting off on this almost as much as I am, I begin to tease myself with the toy. I think Danny is going to give me instructions, telling me where to press and how much pressure to apply, but apart from the slapping of his palm against his cock and the occasional grunt, it's almost possible to forget he's actually there. I start to lose myself in the moment, pushing the vibrator up inside me just a little way before pulling back out to focus on the area just around my clit in the way that's always guaranteed to make me come.

I'm bucking my hips, feeling those little tickly sensations that mean my orgasm can't be too far away, which is precisely when Danny orders me to stop what I'm doing and play the vibrator over my nipples instead. Lifting my T-shirt, I do as he asks, a little reluctantly. But a forfeit's a forfeit, after all, I think, as I feel those delicious spasms die away.

Keeping that thought in mind doesn't make things any easier to bear when Danny tells me I can turn my attention back to my pussy. Again, he watches me take myself right to the brink and again he makes me stop before I get there. I'm sure, as we go into this routine for a third time, that this is when he'll finally allow me to come. I'm wrong. Still unsatisfied, my thighs sticky with a mixture of my own juices and the olive oil, I'm made to put the vibrator away in my bedside drawer. The expression on Danny's face as I do so tells me he is loving being in charge far too much to end the game now.

* * *

I spend the next couple of days in the same state of sweet torment. At Danny's request, I dress in a skirt with no knickers beneath it. It gives him the access he needs to slip a finger up under the hem whenever he feels like it, driving me half-crazy by playing with my clit until I'm on the verge of climaxing and then pulling away. I'm washing the dishes after dinner one evening when he comes up behind me, pressing his hard cock into the cleft of my buttocks and clutching my breasts through my top. He rubs himself against me, letting me know how excited he is, and I reckon he's going to fuck me where I stand. But his self-control is stronger than I might have expected; he's doing just enough to keep me in a state where all I can think about is when he's going to let me come and what it will feel like when I do.

I almost wish he'd put me into some sort of chastity belt; at least that way I would be completely off-limits, waiting patiently till he chooses to release me. What he's done instead is more subtle, more frustrating; my whole being seems concentrated into the area between my legs, and I'm constantly aware of the maddening ache there—an ache that won't be eased until Danny decides the time is right. He could ask me to do anything and I would agree, if only to be allowed to experience that marvelous moment when my orgasm bursts through me.

On the final morning of our holiday, the weather breaks at last. We wake to the sun shining through the thin curtains and the promise of a beautiful day to come. Danny suggests we go out for breakfast and then take that much-delayed walk along the beach. I'm about to roll out of bed so I can shower when he grabs hold of me.

"Not so fast. I want you to take care of this first." He gestures to his erection, standing swollen and proud.

He lies back, hands clasped behind his head and a big smile

on his face as I go to work. I gaze at him submissively as I suck, mouth full of his hot, salty flesh, wondering whether this will be the last day he chooses to play the role of master and whether our sex life will go back to its usual vanilla pattern once we return to the old routine. We certainly won't be having sex on a weekday morning, not with Danny's early start and my long commute, so I give in to the novelty of it, taking even more of my husband's length into my clutching throat.

When he decides I've pleasured him enough, he urges me up onto all fours. I feel his face pushing between my buttocks and his tongue worming into my cunt, licking wetly and opening me up for him.

I'm twitchy with anticipation by the time I feel him sliding into me. For the past few days he's kept me on edge, and even now I don't know whether this will end with both of us coming—or just Danny. Tense and impatient, I push back hard on his cock as it noses its way into me. It's been a long time since I've put so much into a fuck; my breasts are bouncing and the bedsprings are creaking as Danny and I move in a swift, animal rhythm. I can feel the sweat breaking out in little beads in the hollow of my back. Danny's finger finds my clit, rubbing firmly, and yet again I find myself beginning the swift ride to ecstasy. My husband is now as attuned to the pattern of my orgasm as I am, and as he's done so many times over the course of this holiday, he pulls back, letting the intensity fade.

"Don't forget, Jade," he murmurs, "not till I say so."

He thrusts into me harder than ever. His breathing is harsh in my ear, and his fingers are practically crushing my nipples as he toys with them. I'd almost forgotten sex could be so rough, so frantic, and I'm loving every moment of it. Again he turns his attention to my clit, but this time when he starts stroking it he doesn't stop. I'm expecting him to back off, and that's why I'm so startled when instead he says, "Come for me."

The pleasure that has been building and building with no outlet for so many days now comes gushing forth. The tingling, throbbing, pounding feeling that radiates out from my sex to flood the whole of my lower half is so intense that I actually scream. I'm calling out Danny's name, begging him not to stop and using all the foul, filthy words that never pass my lips at any other time. I have truly never had an orgasm like it, and by the time the sensation has passed, I am weak and shaking.

Danny pulls out of me and as I lie on my back, he kneels over me, wanking his cock till the come spurts out of it in big, pearly gobs that decorate my belly, marking me as his.

"So was it worth the wait?" he asks as I smile up at him.

All I can do is nod my head. Even if I could find the words, I don't think I have the energy to speak them.

That evening, as we're making a final tour of the cottage before we set off for home, making sure we're in no danger of leaving anything behind, I find the playing cards lying half-hidden under the living room sofa. Remembering the game of Cheat, I pick them up and flick through them. To my utter disbelief, I realize there really are five aces in the pack, along with a couple of extra sevens and two queen of hearts. On impulse, I slip the cards in my bag. After all, who would have any use for such a rogue deck—apart from someone who has suddenly realized the whole world of possibilities that might spring from another game of forfeits?

WHAT'S IN A NAME?

Jacqueline Applebee

My lover, Eric, pounded into me. The veins on his pale neck stood out as he grunted, moving faster within. I opened my legs wider, arched up to meet his thrusts. My orgasm struck, rocking me hard. My lips, swollen and wet, parted. I cried out as I came.

"Hassan!" A word of bliss escaped me. "Hassan," I sighed. My hips bucked on the mattress and then I collapsed, spent and happy.

Eric looked at me with eyes wide. His mouth hung open. "Hassan?"

"What?" Panic made me freeze.

"You called out someone else's name." Eric peered at me as if he could read the answer on my sweat-covered body. "Who's Hassan?"

"Shit. I'm so sorry." I bit my lip, embarrassed by my mistake. This was an unwritten rule of sex: never mix up names of lovers. Eric and I had been together exclusively for six months, so I had no excuse really. "Just forget it," I said, rather pathetically.

Eric looked down at his cock. He grimaced at his wilting member. "I don't think I can do that." He flopped down on the bed beside me. My afterglow dwindled and then vanished as my lover sighed loudly next to me. I stared up at the ceiling, and then I looked down at the pattern on the sheets as they lay in a heap on the floor, but the paisley swirls could not distract me. I didn't know what to say. It was one of those moments when I wished the ground would just open up and swallow me whole.

"So, this Hassan character..." Eric began.

"I said, forget it."

"He must have been something pretty special." Eric swept a strand of his dark hair from his blue eyes.

"I thought you weren't the jealous type?"

Eric reached over, pinched my nose playfully. "Sweetheart, I know you had plenty of men before we met."

"Are you saying I'm easy?" I snapped.

Eric was silent for a moment. "I'd call you experienced, that's all." He kissed me. I licked over his teeth, traced his lips with mine. I felt desire stir in my belly, replacing the shame I'd felt. "Tell me about this mystery man." Eric ran his tongue over my throat, dotted kisses in the hollow of my collarbone. I smiled; maybe something positive could come out of my slipup after all. I closed my eyes, pictured Hassan the way I'd known him as a young man. I thought of the swaggering dude who made all the girls and most of the boys swoon whenever he walked past. Hassan had stood out in the village where I'd grown up; he'd been an exotically handsome addition to my little corner of rural England where nothing much ever changed until he came. I never found out why his family had ended up there, but I was grateful that they had.

"Hassan was a bit of a legend at school," I started.

"School! You fooled about with this guy at school?"

"No, but I first met Hassan in my final year. Everyone said he was an amazing kisser, but it wasn't until we were older that anything happened between us." Eric sighed with relief. He resumed kissing along my shoulders, making murmuring sounds. I felt his cock twitch against my thigh, growing in size with every passing moment. I was glad he was enjoying the trip down memory lane as much as I was.

"So when you finally got together with this Casanova, what did you do?"

"Oh, nothing much." I gave Eric my best innocent look, which wouldn't fool anyone.

"Are you lying to me?" Eric's voice had suddenly changed; it held a note of menace. He swept his hands over my wrists, which are an unusual erogenous zone of mine, but before I could enjoy the sensation, he gripped them tight, pinning me to the bed. A jolt of fear mixed with lust shot through me. I couldn't be sure if he was really angry or just playing. "Tell me what Hassan did." Eric stared at me. My breath came in short bursts. I struggled, but I could not escape from my position beneath him.

"We just kissed at first when we were at a party," I gulped. "He had this way of devouring me with his kisses. I always felt trapped by his lips and his delicious mouth whenever we smooched."

"Like now?" Eric tugged my hands over my head. I nodded, aware of how my nipples had become hard and aching with need. "What else did you do?"

"He talked dirty; he was the first man who ever spoke to me that way."

"What did he say?" Eric shoved my knees apart with his. He gazed down at my pussy. I knew I was wet, glistening and hungry for his cock.

"He called me a slut." Even saying that word now made a wonderful tremor pass through me. "He said he could smell my cunt, and that it was the best perfume in the world."

"I agree," Eric said with a smile. I arched up wanting him inside me, but Eric increased his grip on my hands. The delicious pressure made me whine. My sensitive wrists felt heavenly. I was desperate for this man.

"Please," I whispered.

"Did Hassan screw you?" Eric ignored my request. "Because I can imagine him slamming into you until you came so hard you screamed his name."

"Hassan didn't have to screw me to give me orgasms that were amazing."

"Liar." Eric moved so he held both my wrists in just one of his large hands. With his free hand, he grabbed one of my legs, and then he lifted it over his shoulder so I was spread wide. He barely gave me a second before he thrust inside. "Tell me what you did." Eric's voice was tight and hard. I wanted to answer him, but my breath was knocked right out of my throat with the force of his thrusts. My cunt gripped Eric's cock, intensifying everything he gave me. My lover squeezed his eyes shut, but as he came, I could have sworn I heard him say something. It sounded for all the world like he had said Hassan's name.

Eric stilled, and then he slumped on top of me. After a moment I felt him reach around, blindly searching for my vibrator that I kept by the side of the bed. I waved him off once I heard the whir begin.

"Don't you want to come again?" he asked, waving the vibrator at me.

"Sure," my voice trailed off as I looked shyly at my man. "Of course…"

Eric looked at me quizzically, until realization dawned on his face. "But you want to come the way you did when you were with Hassan." The calmness in my lover's voice was more than I deserved. "You need to tell me what he did."

I held up my hands. "Hassan would suck on my fingers." My voice was a tiny whisper.

Eric's eyes widened. "You're kidding me!"

"It's the truth. I've always had sensitive hands." I looked away, suddenly ashamed for being such a freak.

"Let me get this straight," Eric said slowly. "You can come from having your hands stimulated?"

"Yes."

Eric raised an eyebrow, but he didn't say anything further. He pulled me to sit astride his lap, and then he placed my thumb into his hot wet mouth. He swirled his tongue over my nail and then lower to the web of flesh where my thumb met my forefinger. My breath stuttered, my clit pulsed and my eyes rolled to the back of my head. Eric flicked on the vibrator, and then he sucked two more fingers into his mouth. He slurped and pulled on them rhythmically. I watched with delight as my fingers disappeared between his lips to be caressed by his talented tongue. I'd never thought of Eric getting together with a man before, but I was certain he'd be a talented cocksucker if he ever did. I increased the speed of my thrusts inside his mouth.

"Hassan," I breathed. "This is Hassan you're sucking on." I hoped I was right about what I'd heard before. I hoped Eric wouldn't hate me for pushing things, but he was just so good at this, I couldn't ignore the opportunity.

I was rewarded when Eric groaned around my fingers. "Hassan," he whispered. His eyes were shut tight. I imagined the men entwined together, two lovers sucking, teasing and pleasuring each other until they both came.

I circled my hips against his and then bucked against the

vibrator as I continued to finger Eric's mouth. Every press of his lips made desire dance from my hands down to my ass. It was like nothing I'd ever experienced. I shuddered as my orgasm shot through me making me quake with the intensity. I toppled down beside my lover, breathlessly happy.

"So…" Eric began quietly after a moment passed. "What we just did." He paused and looked at me hesitantly. "Does this mean I'm going gay?"

I hit him weakly, although I barely had enough strength to move.

"I'd say you were bi-curious, that's all."

"How about try-curious?" he asked with a chuckle.

"You want to try that again?" I managed to sit up in bed. I stroked a finger over Eric's face, running it over his lips. He nipped at it, gently biting the tip.

"Maybe another time." He drew my finger into his mouth once more. A flutter of aftershock made my clit ache deliciously. "Did you keep in contact with Hassan?" he asked.

"We lost touch when I started university."

"That's a shame," Eric sighed. "He sounds like an interesting guy."

"He was, but then I met someone truly special after him."

"Who?" Eric sounded surprised.

"I'm talking about you, silly."

"Of course." Eric pulled me into a sleepy embrace. My finger popped out of his mouth as I snuggled in close. "Of course you were."

CHEMISTRY

Velvet Moore

The smell of science makes me horny.

I narrowly resisted shoving my hands down my pants and rubbing myself to oblivion during my niece's science fair. My stomach dips with pleasure every time someone lights a match. Each July I'm aroused by the vapors of the noise-making novelty fireworks called "snappers." Little do tricksters know that when they crack one on the pavement at my feet, I shiver out of excitement, not fear.

Smell is the sense tied most closely to human memory. So when I sense any use of potassium chlorate—a white, crystalline compound well stocked in science laboratories and often used for combustion—I remember how it feels to have the fire of orgasm sizzle its way through my body and melt a liquid path down my legs. The chemical's odor singes my nostrils and flashes me back to the sensation of a chilly, marble countertop pressed against my back, to the press of fingers digging into my supple thighs, to the slick pressure of rounded glass slipping in and out.

And it's what I remember most about him.

Most scientists that I've met fit the typical stereotypes. Most would rather analyze your genes than pry off your jeans. Yet I suspected that Michael Harrison was capable of much more than stripping me of my pants. With his wavy black hair, broad shoulders and Clark Kent glasses, I believed that stripped of his unassuming attire, he would have something surprising and heroically powerful bulging underneath.

I understood this the first time I shook his hand and caught the scent of chemicals trapped in his clothes and seared into his skin, a smell faint and tangy and far too interesting to be cologne, like the smell of your body after a lengthy swim in a freshly chlorinated pool. I imagined that if I should run my tongue along his perky nipples, my tongue would sizzle as though touched to the tip of a battery.

We needed a scientist to impress the hospital donors with a tour of the lab. I planned to find an excuse to use him.

I spent the following week visiting the lab to get a sense of his work. His area of interest was biochemistry, and I was certainly interested in his chemistry. I came to notice how his hands flexed tightly, fighting against the latex gloves each time he cupped a beaker full of liquid. I watched as he gradually pushed the tip of the lengthy pipette into the stickiness of the gel and ejected its contents. I'd secretly graze my hand across my chest as he pinched and lifted the bell jar by its perky, nipplelike top and used the glassware to create a vacuum.

He stood beside me as an orator while his lab staff performed an experiment in front of eager donors. "Molten potassium chlorate is a strong oxidizing agent that reacts violently with sugar," he explained.

A lab student added a plump, red gummy bear to the white liquid bubbling in a test tube over an open flame. In an instant, the candy ignited, sparking and steaming with the power of an electrical fire and screaming like a train whistle. The sudden pop of energy startled me, and I jumped in reaction as though I had been smacked sharply across the ass with a ruler. Instantly, his hand splayed across my lower back to calm me, a touch that managed to still my nerves and wet my panties.

Quicker than the smoke from the candied combustion, he cleared himself from me and attended diligently to the prospective donors. He ought to have looked like a pauper among princes, he in a rumpled, specked, white lab coat and tattered tennis shoes, among designer suits and patent leather pumps. Yet they clung to his every word, enraptured by the mystifying language of science. As he led the group farther into the lab, I heard him begin to boast about the facility's latest microarray technology. "Good boy," I thought. He had obeyed my coaching and was hitting all of the major speaking points.

After the event, I congratulated him and mentioned that if he felt the need, we could debrief. He told me that he would be working late and that if I stopped by, we would review things.

I agreed.

That evening, I found him bowed over a polarizing light microscope, his pert little ass hidden by the draping of his white lab coat. He stopped upon noticing my arrival.

"I'm just examining some potassium chlorate," he said. "Want to take a look?"

I shifted toward the microscope resting on the waist-high table and bent to peer in the lens. Magnetized, the crystalline powder was transformed into jagged cubes of translucent hues, like miniature ice caps in Technicolor. Although lacking scientific training, I could appreciate beauty enough to admire the hidden complexity of a seemingly simple form.

"It's beautiful," I said.

"Yes, it is," he said, then smoothed the fingers of one hand down my lower back and around the curve of my rear.

I didn't move, and he continued. "I've been meaning to tell you how much I appreciate the short skirts." His fingers continued their downward path and crept between the slit of my skirt. Two fingertips moved forward to slowly stroke the crease of my panties, which rested against my inner thigh. I felt the material soak with a sudden urgency. Unnerved by the speed of the situation, I stood straight and stepped aside. His hands trailed out of reach.

"You think I didn't notice that you've been dressing for me?" he asked, as he moved closer, trapping me between his body and the chest-high countertop of the lab bench, now pressed against my spine. "Safety is important in a lab; that's why it's necessary to wear long pants and flat shoes. I'm glad you choose to live a little dangerously."

I blushed and averted my gaze downward as he called me out.

"Do you know much about potassium chlorate?" he asked.

I squinted as I retook his gaze and shook my head no, undoubtedly revealing my confusion, if not disappointment, by the sudden topic shift.

"It's a fairly common compound, yet incredibly powerful. What's so amazing about it is that it looks unassuming, but when combined with something sweet, it releases a surprising amount of energy." With that, he closed the remaining distance between our bodies and, reaching with one hand, slowly grazed the pad of his thumb across my smooth lower lip. The touch tingled lips above and below my waist.

I watched as he lifted his hand to his mouth and tasted his thumb where my mouth had just been. "I found something sweet...I think we should experiment."

His hot mouth crushed against mine, and I swiftly slid my tongue between his slick lips to pry them open. When his tongue pressed back with equal force, my breath caught and my folds swelled. Eager for pressure, I shoved my hips forward and ground my pelvis against the strong plane of his body. He grabbed my hands, now tangled in his hair, loosened my grip and lowered them to rest against the lab bench ledge. Like a fallen angel, I stood with arms spread wide, awaiting his command. His nimble fingers made quick work of my shirt's buttons and my bra, and he encircled my right breast with his slick mouth.

As he feasted to the right, he pinched my left nipple, pausing only to roll it between his fingers like a fine cigar. The groans that escaped his muffled mouth made me raw with want. Then he suddenly pulled back. I reached out to draw him back in, but he again pressed my hands down. I was eager to see the lengthy muscle that had so eagerly been pushed against my aching middle, but he lowered to his knees without disrobing. He gripped the fronts of my thighs beneath my skirt and spread my legs farther. He pushed the skirt up around my waist, tucking the bottom into the waistband to keep it put. Down slipped my soaked panties as he pried them along my legs and tossed them aside. A hand cupped possessively at my swollen sex, his palm spreading my lips, pressing against my throbbing clit, fingers toying along the crease of my rear. He met my eyes and showed a sly smile.

Removing his hand from my body, he reached into the deep pocket of his white lab coat and then pulled out a glass test tube. I gripped the lab bench a little tighter. The slender cylinder slipped easily onto his middle finger. His sly expression disappeared and a look of intense concentration took its place as he leaned forward and leisurely ran the weighty tip of his tongue from the bottom of my soaked sex to the tip of my throbbing clit, making sure to increase pressure during his ascent.

I felt his tongue flick vigorously over my clit while he slipped into me with his glass-shrouded finger. The tube glided easily along my slick folds, and its rounded tip bumped against all the right places. The combination of his tongue and the tool shot jagged, electric currents between my legs, causing me to twitch, my legs to wobble, my heart to race, my breath to become shallow, moans to escape, my head to roll back, my hands to tighten their grip and my mind cloud with the sharp thrill of sexual release. Fingers of his free hand gripped my ass when the height of my orgasm hit, causing me to groan out an "Oh, god," that echoed throughout the lab, and I pushed his mouth away to abate the overwhelming intensity.

He slipped out of me, rose from his knees and stood silently, watching as my body calmed. Once my breath had slowed, I raised my head, attempting to fight the postpeak weariness.

Wanting to please him and willing for more, I grabbed the waistband of his pants, unbuttoned and unzipped them and pushed them down and off his sturdy legs. Next, I headed for the buttons of his collared shirt and painstakingly attempted to undo them all.

Sensing my lingering fatigue, he assisted and then finally removed his boxers, letting his solid shaft stand free. He stood there mostly naked, draped in his lab coat, like a Central Park flasher with a PhD.

Reaching out, I coiled his cock in my hand and he groaned when I began tugging with my tightened grip. With equal force he clenched the wrist of my offending hand and pulled me off. Taking advantage of my surprise and of his hold, he spun me around and pressed me forward against the lab bench so that its edge that once pushed along my spine now settled against my abs. Like a yogi in a bow of submission, I stretched my arms forward to steady myself, carelessly pushing aside bottles, scales and other miscellaneous laboratory equipment. I was poised for sexual satisfaction, not for scientific measurement.

He yanked at my hips and I shuffled to a wider stance. His knuckles bumped along my crease as his hand guided his powerful cock inside me, slipping in deeply and filling me like a man should and in a way that glass could never match. "Oh, shit, you're tight," he said with a groan. I clenched around him for added affect.

The pumping started easily at first, long and steady, allowing my faded excitement to bubble back to the surface, like liquid in a beaker over low heat. In this eased pace, I was able to press my pelvis forward enough to knock my clit against the brass handle of the drawer beneath me. The pressing of his hips repeatedly shoved his cock in and out of me and the handle against my center, bringing it to a sensitive, plump peak.

With my female firearm triggered, I felt myself grow wetter with every intrusion, his pleasured moans serving as a catalyst to my excitement. Now edgy with pleasure and eager for speed, I shoved my ass toward him, drawing him in deeper and signaling my desire. His pace quickened and he pummeled my soaking pussy with plunged force. The sound of my ass smacking against his skin and the flaps of his coat ticking against the bench added to the rising symphony of our sex.

My shallow breathing accelerated and the electricity that resonated between my thighs prickled swiftly to my limbs, signaling my oncoming climax. I pulled his hand from my hip and used his fist to bite back the intensity. But the taste of his coppery skin coupled with his pumping overwhelmed me; my body shuddered as I came with electric force. He pulled his hand from my mouth, yanked my body up from my sprawled pose and with rapid fire released his hot come into me.

We leaned together as our breathing calmed and the heat of our bodies cooled. I turned and switched my resting place from his chest to the countertop and looked upon him with a glazed gaze.

He gradually buttoned his lab coat and once completely cloaked, he advanced with equal lethargy.

"What did you learn from our little experiment?" he asked, using a finger to draw lazy yet tantalizing figure eights around my belly button.

I grabbed the wrist of the wandering hand, cupped his palm against my breast and responded, "It's all about chemistry."

THE CHAIR

Lolita Lopez

The chair was a thing of sumptuous decadence: Sleek lines. Gleaming onyx wood. That ever-so-plush leather. From the first moment she'd spied the chair, Lily had desperately wanted to sink down into its sensual embrace. It had called to her, whispering naughtily in her ear and promising a sexual experience to top all others. Even now, all these weeks later, just staring at the chair sent jittery waves through her belly.

Her vivid imagination shot into overdrive. She could almost feel the cool kiss of leather against her naked skin and the tight clinch of the padded cuffs around her ankles and wrists. The thought of being bound to the chair, helpless and completely at Cal's mercy, made her pussy pulse with need. Sticky wetness seeped between her bare thighs from sheer anticipation.

"Sit."

Cal's instruction sent white-hot shock waves through her core. Lily's nipples stood at attention. She inhaled a shuddery breath and took a tentative step forward. Skimming her fingertips over the smooth wooden arm, Lily appreciated the beauty and craftsmanship of the chair. Only a hedonist like Cal would think to commission such a hybrid piece of furniture. Part bondage device and part sex toy, it was legendary among his rather kinky circle of friends.

Before Cal, Lily had only dabbled in the lightest of kink: A silk scarf binding her wrists to a headboard. An ice cube between her lover's lips gliding over the swell of her breast. A few stinging smacks on her bottom in the heat of passion.

But then Cal had appeared in her life and introduced her to the sometimes painful but always exhilarating world of BDSM. That first night he'd broached the subject, Cal had taken her to his playroom and talked her through the various toys and implements. When he'd shown her the chair sitting in the corner on a raised platform, Lily's curiosity had been piqued. What was hidden beneath the panels spanning the distance between the chair's legs? And why did the platform require a power source? In that instant, she'd decided to accept the experience Cal offered and earn the privilege to sit on his prized piece.

"Lily."

Cal's prompt brought her back to the present. Fingers trembling with trepidation, she stepped onto the dais. Lily turned to face her lover and slowly sank down onto the wide seat. Her bare feet dangled above the platform. Her belly quivered with apprehension. She suddenly felt so young and inexperienced. Perhaps that was part of the design. Cal seemed to enjoy throwing her composure off kilter before every scene. There was something about embracing the unknown and giving her complete trust to him that amplified the experience and eventual release.

Perched on the chair, Lily eyed Cal as he moved out of the shadows. Tonight he remained fully dressed, a stark contrast to her vulnerable state and a clear reminder of his absolute control of the situation. He pocketed his platinum cufflinks and slowly rolled up the sleeves of his crisp shirt. Lily licked her lips and pressed her knees tightly together. She gripped the arms of the chair as Cal moved closer. Their gazes clashed as he wrapped the leather cuffs over her wrists. He didn't break their mutual stare as he picked up the remote control and adjusted the tilt of the chair's reclining back, pushing her hips up slightly.

He set aside the remote and knelt in front of the chair. Cal's warm breath tickled her shins as he grazed his lips over her skin and placed kisses along the curves of her knees. He buckled her ankles to the legs of the chair, forcing her thighs wide open and baring the smoothly waxed lips of her cunt to his appreciative gaze. She recognized the fiery gleam in his eyes. He'd seen the evidence of her arousal, the shiny juices seeping from her and coating her skin.

Cal brushed his knuckles over her sex. "You always get so wet."

"Only for you."

Her breathless words brought a smile to his face. Cal leaned forward and nuzzled his nose in her dripping pussy. His pointed tongue swiped her slit, flicking the stiff nub aching so desperately for his touch. Lily tried to arch her hips to meet his prodding tongue but the bonds held her in place. She whimpered in protest but Cal simply wiped his mouth with the back of his hand and backed away from her.

Lily's eyes widened as Cal removed the cloth covering the small table standing just to his left and revealed a variety of floggers, clamps and straps. She swallowed hard. He was going to drag this out and make her earn every mind-blowing orgasm.

Air hissed through her teeth at the first heavy thud of suede ribbons against her breasts. Cal wielded the flogger with the efficiency of a true master, his strikes caressing her naked skin. She arched into the flicks, loving the sensations the gentle warm-up swats evoked. Tendrils of arousal blossomed in the pit of her belly. Heat spread across her chest and down her softly sloped stomach.

Soon Cal switched to a stiffer flogger. Lily cried out at the first stinging swat of the rigid leather tongues against her sensitized skin. The leather grazed her pebbled nipples and licked down the curved plane of her tummy. She sucked in her breath and tried to pull back to avoid the incessant flicks but it was no use. The chair's tilted back made it impossible for her to escape Cal's flogging.

Prickly heat erupted wherever the leather ribbons touched. Cal increased the tempo of his swats and allowed the stinging fingers to fall a little harder each time. When she felt the flogger's kiss moving lower, Lily shivered. She yelped at the first slap of leather against her bare pussy. With her ankles pinned and thighs spread wide, Cal had total access to the dewy center of her sex and apparently had no intention to spare her most tender place.

Her first instinct was to shout out their safeword but she shoved away the urge, determined to conquer this new and frightening sensation. She panted and tensed before every smack of the flogger. Her hips shifted from side to side in a desperate attempt to escape Cal's next swat.

And then she felt it.

Behind every stinging kiss there was the most delicious ripple vibrating her clit. Lily concentrated on that wonderfully electrifying sensation. In no time at all, she'd lifted her hips to meet every downward fall of the flogger's leather tongues. This was the place she'd learned to accept as a submissive. The sweet agony of pleasure and pain threw her senses into overdrive. Every nerve in her body flared as she hovered on the brink of explosion.

When Cal stopped unexpectedly, Lily groaned with displeasure and immediately knew she'd broken one of their established rules. During these games they played, her position was simply to accept and never to dictate. Cal clicked his teeth and shook his head. Breathing hard and trying desperately to ignore the uncomfortable pulse of her pussy, Lily warily watched her lover to see what punishment he would choose.

As if sensing her stare, Cal selected a length of black silk and applied a blindfold. Her eyesight lost, Lily waited with bated breath, her body humming nervously. Cal's fingers drifted over her breasts. In the next second, she experienced that all too familiar bite of a clothespin. A series of the wooden torture devices followed along the plump swell of her breasts.

As she acclimated to the pinching sensation, Lily felt her bottom drop a bit. With a push of a button, Cal had removed a center strip of the seat. It noiselessly slid down into the base and presented Cal with complete access to her naughty bits. Exposed to his mercy, Lily could only wonder what might come next. Her clit was still swollen and just a few flicks away from sending her into a screaming orgasm.

She stilled as Cal drew closer, his body heat penetrating her skin. His warm breath buffeted her neck. His sandalwood scent filled her nose. She moaned hungrily as his slippery fingers glided between the lips of her cunt and slid even lower to the pucker hidden there. She surrendered to his probing, allowing his fingers to relax her ass for his inevitable intrusion. Before Cal, Lily had refused to even consider that particular sex act. It was wrong and dirty.

Cal had shown her she'd been absolutely right. Anal sex was dirty—deliciously and naughtily so. And now she couldn't get enough.

His fingers disappeared. A moment later, the blunt tip of a

dildo prodded her ass. So that's what was hidden beneath the seat of the chair! Cal had mounted sex toys in the compartment there. She could hear the whir of a motor as the dildo rose and fell.

Lily yielded to the pressure of the nudging dildo. It slipped inside and stretched her ring with each shallow thrust. Cal's lips were on her neck, setting her skin alight with goose bumps as the motorized dildo fucked her ass. His mouth drifted lower, skimming between her breasts and peppering a line of kisses down to her navel. His tongue circled her belly button before zigzagging right down to her dripping cunt. Hands on her inner thighs, he traced her folds with his tongue.

She was on fire. The dueling sensations of being taken by the dildo and licked by Cal threatened to send her over the edge. She tugged on her wrist cuffs, fingers itching to rake through Cal's hair, to hold his head there, just there, as she came against his mouth. She was close; so very, very close.

Cal's tongue disappeared abruptly. Lily cried out and pumped her hips as the dildo penetrated her bottom again and again. He'd stolen her orgasm and she hated him for it. At the same time, she wanted to beg him to return, to flick his tongue against her clit just one more time. But he'd only laugh at her and find a new way to tease. Her predicament was simultaneously infuriating and thrilling.

Shaking with need, Lily blinked wildly as the blindfold was whipped free. She focused on Cal's face, his stony expression betraying none of the amusement and pleasure she knew he must have been experiencing at her expense. His touch was surprisingly gentle as he caressed her cheek and pressed a kiss to her mouth. He nipped at her lower lip. "Do you want to come?"

"Yes." Her strangled reply filled the room. "Please."

The corner of his mouth lifted. "Soon."

And then he was backing away from her and picking up his

remote control again. The dildo buried deep inside her ass paused and a new silicone phallus prodded her pussy. She wiggled until it slid into place. Double penetration was fairly new to Lily. Cal had been training her over the last few weeks to accept both his cock and a dildo. Now she understood why.

With alternating thrusts, the dildos drove into her repeatedly. When Cal added another toy to the mix, an intimidating black wand with a tennis-ball-sized vibrator mounted on top, Lily went wild. There was no controlling her reaction. The buzzing ball pressed against her clit sent vibrating waves through her belly and down into her thighs. Her body tensed, toes curling, fingers clenching as she climaxed so hard she feared blacking out.

"That's it, love. Come for me."

She couldn't deny him, not now, not ever. Undulating against her bonds, Lily rode out the shocking waves of her orgasm. Every thrust of the cocks amplified the experience until it was too much. She begged Cal to stop, to take away the vibrator, but even as she pleaded for mercy, she couldn't bring herself to utter their safeword. The primitive, sex-crazed whore lurking deep inside her, the very essence of her id, had been set free. Lily was helpless to stop it now. This was going just as far as Cal cared to take it.

Just as Lily surged into another orgasm, Cal picked up a flogger and expertly flicked the leather ribbons against the clothespins clinging to her breasts. They snapped free and clattered to the ground. Lily shrieked as intensely sharp pain mixed with the unbelievable ecstasy of her forced climax exploded in her core. The flogger slapped against her flushed skin again and again. Her mind reeled as she swung from one extreme to the other. Pain. Pleasure.

Lily's orgasms changed from separate events to one long and

unending oscillation of bliss. She barely registered the disappearance of the vibrator and dildo that had been stimulating her pussy. The rubber cock remained in her ass, its speed kicked up a few notches. Cal's fingers replaced the other dildo. He hovered over her, his knee wedged against hers on the lip of the chair, and finger-fucked her cunt until she thought she just might die.

"You know what I want." His fingers bumped her G-spot relentlessly. His thumb massaged tight circles around her inflamed clit.

She shook her head. Embarrassment stained her cheeks even as she hovered on the brink of coming again. "I can't."

"You can." His calm tone pierced the fever pitch. "And you will."

And she did. Like before, she found it impossible to deny Cal. She surrendered completely to the almost irritating urge his thrusting fingers evoked. Screaming like a banshee, Lily squirted all over his hand, her juices running along his wrist and forearm. Cal growled with appreciation as she skyrocketed to a new place, a place of such intense ecstasy she couldn't think, could hardly breathe. She was simply a vessel for the most rapturous sensations imaginable.

At some point, Lily blacked out, her mind simply unable to process the overwhelming explosion of orgasmic wonder. When she came to, her wrists and ankles had been freed from their bonds. Cal knelt between her thighs and lapped languidly at her, his talented tongue gathering her slick cream and teasing her into awareness.

With a heavy sigh, Lily reached down and ran her fingers through his fine hair. In the gentle moments like this, Cal showed her just how much he truly loved her. The contrast between this Cal and the man who sometimes subjected her to painful sensual tortures was as different as night and day—just as the girl who allowed Cal to dominate her was nothing like the no-nonsense, ball-breaking Lily who lectured on feminism to a hall of half-asleep undergrads three days a week. Theirs was a complex relationship and one she wouldn't have traded for anything in the world.

"So," Cal said, his lips brushing her inner thigh, "what do we think of my little contraption?"

Lily gave a purr of satisfaction. With an impish smile curving her mouth, she bent down and captured his lips. "I think we should have one built for you."

Cal's eyes lit up at her suggestion. He grinned and nipped at her belly. "You'd have to shine a hell of a lot of boots before you'd earn enough points to take the reins over me."

"What can I say?" She shrugged and gave him a saucy wink. "I'm turning out to be quite the glutton for punishment."

FIXING
THE PIPES

Susie Hara

Bobbie savored these few minutes before bed when she could read, uninterrupted, in the peacefulness of the quiet house; the children asleep, Scott working on the computer. It was Friday night, just her and her book. She turned the page. If only she could stay awake long enough to read. She felt her eyelids droop. Scott appeared in the doorway. It was early for him to be coming to bed. He closed the door behind him. Uh-oh. He had The Look. *Mmm.* But she wanted to read her book; she'd been waiting all day.

"I'm reading this really great book, Scottie."

"Oh, yeah?" He came over and stroked between her fingers where she was holding the book and then he stroked the book.

"Mmm," he said, and started licking her hand.

"Could you go away and come back in a few minutes?" she said, wanting him, but wanting her long-awaited reading time more.

"Oh! Go away! Come back! I see! I will, indeed, Madame. I will go—hence—now I will henceforth go forth and return!"

he said with a flourish and a bow and then was gone.

Jeez, Bobbie thought, *that wasn't what I meant.* She kept reading as quickly as she could knowing that whatever he was up to, it was going to be imminently distracting. She got in several more pages before the door opened. God, where did he get that outfit? He was dressed in a dark blue workman's jumpsuit with RICK sewn on in orange thread. He was carrying his toolbox.

"Ma'am, I'm here to fix the pipes," Scott whispered.

"Oh, okay," Bobbie said. "The bathroom's down the hall."

"I'm not here to fix the bathroom," he said, eyeing her nipples through her nightgown.

"Should I show you where the kitchen is, then?"

"Ma'am, the plumbing I need to fix is in here. Yes," he whispered as he closed the bedroom door behind him, softly. "The pipes are in that wall, over near the bed. I'm afraid I need to open up the wall and work on those pipes."

"Oh, I don't know. That sounds pretty messy. My husband's coming home soon and he…he…" Here she paused. "He won't want the wall all torn apart."

"I assure you, this won't take long." Scott came around to the wall next to her and got his tools out. "I hope you don't mind my asking, but what's your name?"

"Um. Gloria. My name is Gloria. And your name is Rick, right?"

"Well, I know it says Rick on my overalls, but actually I got these from the guy who had the job before me, see, so my name is…um…uh…Hunk."

"*Hunk?* Your name is *Hunk?*"

"Yes, that's right." He swung his hammer and knocked a hole through the sheetrock.

"What the fuck are you doing?" she hissed. "You'll wake the children."

"Gloria, I'm awfully sorry, but it's the only way to get to the pipes," he grinned.

He leaned over and softly placed the head of the hammer on the skin just below her collarbone, where her nightgown fell open. He caressed her with the cool metal head, drawing patterns that sloped gradually down toward her breasts. She was breathing hard. She looked him in the eye as he continued his circling, until the hammer rested in the valley between her breasts.

"It has been *so long* since I have felt a hammer between my breasts," she said. She watched the corners of Scott's mouth twitch, as he stifled a laugh. He methodically moved the hammer to her left nipple, moving it around and around, which caused her to shiver and close her eyes. Her book dropped to the floor. It was quiet for a time, while he traced the cool metal around each of her nipples, which were now puckered and pointing straight up. She grabbed him and pulled him on top of her in one motion.

"Oh, Hunk! Fix me! Fix my pipes and my—" she stopped cold. The door to the room was open and two small figures stood in the doorway. One toddler and one six-year-old, both in long nightgowns, with big eyes, clutching their teddy bears.

"Are you playing that game?" Rowena said. Both girls came slowly into the room, smiling as they quietly advanced. "Daddy, are you fixing something? Is that why you have that hammer?" she added.

"Yes, Daddy's fixing something, but you have to go back to bed. Remember how we talked about this before? Come on, back to bed for both of you," Scott said.

"Can't we play, too? I know how to use a hammer," Rowena said.

"Ammuh, ammuh!" Hannah said.

Scott took each child by the hand and led them back to their room.

Bobbie groaned. *Probably scarring them for life,* she thought. *Oh, well. I guess they'll have to work it out in therapy when they're older, just like the rest of us did.* She smiled to herself.

Scott came back.

"Lock it," she whispered urgently.

He locked the door behind him and jumped back on top of her, resuming his hammer tracing, but now he was beginning to move the hammer lower.

"Gloria, darling, if I am to fix you, I must remove the covering to your...your pipes," he said.

"Oh, Hunk, I mustn't. I really mustn't. My husband will be home soon."

"There's plenty of time. I know when he comes home. Don't worry." Scott got some scissors out of his toolbox and slowly cut her nightgown off her.

She rolled her eyes at him. She knew he had never liked this nightgown. "Oh, oh," she sighed.

He moved the hammerhead down the length of her body, arriving at her mound, making figure eights with the cool steel. As the figure eights descended, he began to delicately open her labia with the hammerhead.

"Hunk!" She grabbed his cock underneath the fabric of the jumpsuit. "Hammer me with your rod of love!" At this, Scott could not restrain a guffaw, but he quickly regained his composure and ripped off his jumpsuit, under which he was naked and his rod of love was at attention. He rubbed it against her vulva.

"Oh, Gloria, ma'am," he said, moving down and settling his face between her legs. "As much as I want to slide my hot rod of love inside you, I always lubricate the area before going in and making repairs. It's a sign of good workmanship." He lifted his head and looked at her solemnly. "I would be ashamed if I did not practice my trade with the utmost skill and"—he paused here for effect—"respect. Respect for the sacred tunnel of love, the entrance to the inner workings of your temple." He put his tongue inside her labia and slid it up and down and around, below the base of her clit.

It was quiet. His hands slid up to her breasts and flicked her nipples. She was breathing hard, would probably be moaning if it weren't for the children.

She heard the hammer clatter on the floor. He put his fingers inside her cunt as he continued tonguing her in the way that only he knew so well. She felt a wave coming on, rolling over her, and she heard herself whisper a moan and then the wave spread all through her as she bucked on his fingers and the sensations broke over the crest. He kept going.

"Don't move," she whispered. He stopped. She lay there panting hard.

Scott moved up and kissed her with his wet lips, smiled and whispered, "Now I can go in and do my job with the knowledge that I have practiced good workmanship." He plunged his cock into her welcoming cunt. She met him with a powerful thrust back and then rolled him over so they were both on their sides, each thrusting and meeting the other in the middle.

"Hunk. You really know how to grease those pipes."

Then she felt another wave roll over her and she let out a whispered "Ah," a long silent moan, and Scott was looking at her with that half-lidded look, pressing and pushing into her again and again.

She closed her eyes in a kind of trance. *We could do this forever*, she thought. She opened her eyes and kissed him, a major tongue-down-your-throat kind of kiss, and then he had this look of surprise on his face like he was being taken over by something and he wasn't quite ready, like he wanted to prolong it, but she knew he was holding back more for her pleasure than for his, so she grabbed his butt and pressed him into her.

"Scott. You feel so good inside me. So right."

And he came.

They lay there, side by side, breathing hard into the quiet of the house.

She pulled away and looked him in the eye. "Hunk. You better leave before my husband gets home." She giggled.

"You know what?" he whispered into her ear. "Don't worry about your husband. I fixed him good. He won't be back until Monday. If ever."

SHARE

Dusty Horn

At the risk of sounding like a sex toy reviewer, I must confess that the first time I saw this toy, my G-spot started to drool, slack jawed, mesmerized like a preadolescent boy wired with that visual predilection we hear so much about, seeing pink in a magazine for the very first time, suddenly confused with a sickening, indescribable longing to have that uncanny flesh wrapped around his dick.

My roommate works at the farmer's market, and our home is filled with stacks and stacks of long, flat cardboard boxes packed with whatever is in season. We live in produce abundance. At stone fruit time, I walk the earth with sticky syrup crystallizing on my chin. I can't help but dream of pussy every time I bury my face in vibrant peach juice, but I may just be thinking of that LL Cool J video. Day in, day out, we slurp down so much pink and white and orange flesh bursting from taut, furry skin that in a search for oral texture variety, my other roommate discovers and recommends pit sucking. Even I am amazed by what a hippie pervert I can be when the hard, porous ridges of the peach pit against my tongue remind me of my own G-spot.

What an unsexy term: G-spot. It's bad enough that the anatomy in question is cursed to hide in the cave of my pussy like a bat hanging upside down. It's not even clinical or conservative, because as we all know sometimes official words are hotter than slang; G-spot sounds like a *Cosmo* bullshit rumor, like pop psychology. Can we get some dirty colloquialism in here, stat? Rub my clit! Suck my dick! Tongue my asshole! Press my G-spot? Oh, no, no, no. Urethral sponge? Forget about it.

Now, some G-spot toys are vibrators with a slight curve. Thanks for the thought, guys, but someone like me thinks *Yeah! A toy designed for G-spots!*—and then she sticks it in and even wiggles it around some and then she sighs and says, *Well, maybe somebody's, but not mine.*

I've seen double dongs before, novel and awkward, but I can tell just by looking at the contours of this toy that it wants to fill the negative form my G-spot makes and bridge the schism between my peach pit and your cervix.

My pussy wants to undulate on this toy, my pussy wants to grab and yank it, my pussy wants to drag itself across this bulb.

The first time I put the bulbous, lima bean–shaped base inside me, my pussy swallowed it up like a meal it had been waiting its entire penetrative existence to chomp. From the base wedged in my cunt emerged a long, thin, elegant, black cock, lunging out from my crotch very much like it owned the place. I lay on my back on my bed and stroked my new cock with your spit, watching you watching me. Your androgyny flickered across your naked shape—strong shoulders, gumdrop nipples. And then you fell on me throat first, wrapping your lips around my fresh new extension.

I was a cocksucker getting my cock sucked.

Your eyes rolled back in your head as you put on a show for me, pushing, pulling, sucking, drooling. The nerves of your tongue, your lips, your gums did not connect with my nerves, but I felt the ballistic force of your lost inhibitions. Each yank of your head smashed deliciously against my G-spot. I spasmed and contracted, and come welled up around the base of my cock instead of through it and out it, like a loose garden hose faucet.

In my mind's eye, my G-spot resembles a walnut shell embedded in the upper wall, the ceiling, of my pussy. After fifteen-odd years of beating my clit like it owes me money, I have redirected my orgasmic attentions to that chandelier. If I could, I would tongue it like you tongue peanut butter stuck to the roof of your mouth.

Man, it's true, I got dick envy. It's almost too predictable for a twenty-first-century queer alpha female to admit. Problem is, transitioning genders wouldn't satisfy my urge, 'cause what I want is less to present and be perceived as a man than to have experienced coming up as one.

I want to be the man-child with the uncontrollable urge; I want to feel my dick mutate, like the Incredible Hulk bursting outta his clothes, the way my nipples go from puffy to diamond-cutting. I want to write my name in the snow in yellow and on your fucking face in translucent white goo. This will never be my lot. I had given up on having a dick.

But with the right tool and a little imagination…

It's almost too good to be true, this dick that emerges from my cunt. This delightful bulb with which I am having a love affair feels like a real attachment, an almost disgustingly cyber-punk possibility, something that is going to clone cells and attach to my G-spot.

People speak so fondly of their clits as dicks, but this is my monstrous G-spot extension. This is the broadsword of my real power. When I hump and grind on you, this is the prop I wish was there. It's more than a little bit grotesque, Cronenbergesque, a monolith emerging from a gaping gash.

You never know how much arousal has to do with power and gender and control and debasement, as much as it does with connecting nerve endings, until a silicone phallus, jutting statuesquely from your crotch, disappears into a pretty face. You feel a surge of what can only be testosterone because I swear to god, it makes you feel like solving problems with violence and being incredibly insensitive. How else can I explain the need to *fuck the face* of someone I love, to behave in the most despicable porn fashion, grunting and grabbing and jackhammering like a goddamn animal?

So getting my dick sucked inspires testosterone, yes, but also an exultant *Eureka!* sensation—*this* is the real gender. I am exorcizing the demon gender by exercising its physical body. I am putting on the gender act and it's *hot!* It's hot to paint masculinity in broad strokes. You recognize my behavior as male and you recognize me as not male: a simple yet effective formula. Gender is phony. Gender is every bit this double-sized dildo. Gender is much less a functional anatomical reality attached to our bodies and brains than just another useful tool to get off.

Now, alone, on my back on the bed, I visualize you, my ladylove. I am putting on a show for myself, the jerk-off show, my favorite program. And behind the scenes my little bulb is working away. A tug of war—I pull on the dick with my hand and counter-clench around the bulb with my pussy wall. *Where do you think you're going?*

Yeah, this is the perfect dick for you, isn't it, you little faggot? You can tell when it pounds into you it's the physical manifestation of my lust, my pussy turned inside out. My pussy is the foundation of this tower, the conduit between your insides and mine. This is the right dick for the kinda faggot you are. Sure as shit is the right kinda dick for the kinda faggot I am.

I do everything I always dreamed of doing with a dick. I pistol-whip your cheek. I straddle your chest and pull up the head of my cock. My hips pulse down so gravity combines with the whipping effect to slam your tits and sternum hard. And inside it springs up onto me and I damn near convulse. I flip you over and do the same smacking to your creamy ass. *Thwack! Thwack! Taptaptaptap THWACK.* I rub my cock lasciviously over your body, all your erogenous zones.

I get a good long look at that pussy. I could stare at pussy all day. Your pussy helps me to understand why men shell out all their money just so a girl will turn around and touch her toes. I eye the vaselike symmetry of your inner thighs, fat folds tucked and huddled.

I spread my fingers wide, place my hand on your ass and lift the skin tightening across your muscles, and the flap of your labia pulls reluctantly away; it's an anomaly, a novelty in a body and personality that is so uncommonly masculine. My love for you is located in your pussy as you swallow your pride, arch your back and offer yourself to me. The contrast between your boyish charms and this intoxicating sticky elegant peach is more beautiful than anything that has ever corresponded. Fuck correspondence. The only things that should be corresponding are my dick and your cervix.

In my fantasy I slam you harder than you would allow me, and that is what fantasy is for, after all. I get the most wonderful show now; the show of you enjoying yourself, getting off, getting fucked. Whatever it is that fills us with the love of being penetrated, you are feeling it now, and whatever inspires our fascination with watching others love to love the love that loves is washing over me now.

The side of your face is smushed against the sheet and your arms are flopped to the sides. You are wailing a single note, and too bad I don't have perfect pitch or I would write you a song in that key. Our pussies have a tin-can telephone now.

Your finger starts to stir your clit in countermotion to my grind. There is no biological imperative to your come.

I am every man I ever imagine fucking me, fucking you.

And now I am coming hard and I don't hear you complaining about the lack of jizz inside you. If I pulled out and jerked onto your face I don't think you'd pout as you licked around trying to find something salty. Inside my body, I am coming, and this tool behaves like a conduit, sending my come to your insides. My G-spot shudders. Every thrust presses and rubs against it, making it pulsate, making it quake. The chandelier is shaking in the earthquake.

My pussy sorely surrenders the bulb of my toy. I toss it over the edge of the bed, roll over and fall asleep.

HURDLES

Rowan Elizabeth

Did you come?"

Alan looks up from between my legs, hopeful.

"God, baby. That felt really good." I run my hand through his curly hair as I lift my head up from the pillow. I smile. "Really good."

"But did you come?"

I hate this part. Alan and I have only been sleeping together for a month, but he has a monkey on his back. He just can't get me off orally. And it's not for lack of trying.

"No, sweetie. I didn't." He looks dejected. "But it was so exciting. Your mouth felt so good on me."

"Good. Just good?"

I can't win this. And it's my hang-up, too. I feel like there's something I'm just not doing right. Maybe if I tighten my legs a little more or squeeze my eyes shut harder, then we'd get there together.

I sigh. "Baby, I was so close that time. Really. There's just something that's not clicking." I smile at my lover. "Come up here and make love to me."

Alan smiles back, but I know he's going to obsess on it. I'll have to distract him. I grab him by the shoulders and guide him up to kiss me. I wiggle my hips against his cock and reach down to stroke him.

I love the feel of Alan's cock in my hand. He has the most perfect penis I've ever seen. His length is exactly right to hit my G-spot when he rams it into me and his girth fills me completely. Plus, he feels delightful in my mouth.

As I stroke Alan with my hand, he moans, a deep low sound, and starts moving his hips to my rhythm. I press his cockhead against my wet pussy and he pushes in. My eyes roll back. I love this part: the first moment he enters me. He moves into me slowly, pulls back and then goes just a bit farther. It's delicious when he's fully in me and our bodies come together. Alan's cock glides in and out of me so smoothly. I'm so very wet from his mouth and fingers. How can I be so wet and so far along and not come?

As we finish, I can't help but wonder what I need to do differently next time.

"Maggie, he's the most tremendous lover," I tell my best friend. "But we have this hurdle and, even when we're not trying to jump it, it's still there staring us in the face."

"What in the hell are you talking about?"

"Even if we don't try for the big O, we're thinking about it. It's becoming weird."

"Have you gotten frigid on me, Dana?" Maggie laughs.

"It's not funny, you bitch! I really want to come!"

"Well, you know you can, right?"

"I always have before." I think back to the first lover who

could drive me off the edge of the bed chasing my orgasms. He's the one who taught me how to come. "I feel like I need to be taught again."

"Maybe you're not the one who needs to be taught," Maggie suggests.

"Mags! I know he knows what he's doing. It's just getting his talents to work for my needs."

"Then tell him what's not working," she says.

"How do I do that without stomping all over his ego?"

"Alan is a good man and he's crazy about you. Just tell him what you need. He'll listen."

I get back to my apartment late, feed the cats and take a shower. I catch myself staring as I think about coming and how to make it happen. And happen a lot. Frankly, I need it. It keeps me sane.

Drying off, I check myself out in the mirror. *Thirty never looked so good,* I laugh to myself. My dark hair hangs wet against my face and I trail my hands over my body.

What do I need?

I run my palm over my right breast and nipple. It feels nice, but just nice. So I give my nipple a good squeeze. That could work, though I know my nipples are not the path to orgasm for me.

I pad through my apartment to my bedroom and dig around in my bottom dresser drawer. I find my favorite vibrating dildo and a tattered copy of a Portia de Costa book and make my way to my bed. It's a little section of the book where the heroine gets buggered for the first time that always gets to me.

I begin gently rubbing my pussy as I read, dipping my fingers into the folds and bringing out the wetness. I run my finger over my clit, barely making contact, and it makes me shiver. It's so easy to do for myself.

Then it hits me. I just need to remember what gets me going

in detail and then guide Alan through it. *Show him,* I decide. *I just need to show him.*

I slide my curved dildo inside of me and begin rubbing in earnest. I come with bursts of color behind my eyes and a plan hatching in my head.

I open my front door to Alan. His smile melts me. "Hello, handsome."

The moment he's inside, he holds and kisses me. Deep, wet kisses. He kisses like no one else as he runs his hands over my face and into my hair. I love this. I tell him so with my tongue.

I could start dinner and we could obsess over what would come after. But, instead, I lead Alan to the sofa and push him down. "Take off your clothes."

Alan loves my blow jobs and I love doing it for him. He laughs at me when I tell him that I've never been a blow job girl. After an old lover told me that he didn't care for them, I quit. I was sure it was my technique, or lack thereof. Alan, however...

"Damn, baby," he murmurs as I take the head of his cock in my mouth. I lick the ridge and dip my head down to take him in. I stroke his cock with the wet heat of my mouth. I go down as deep as I can and hear, "God." Alan digs his hands into my hair and tilts my head up to look at him. I open my mouth and lick up the shaft as I look into his eyes.

My hand wraps around his base and I take him from my mouth. I rub his cock against my wet lips and across my face and am rewarded with a deep sigh and Alan dropping his head back on the sofa. I pull him back into my mouth.

I can suck on Alan for a long time, but I have my plan and I intend to get him just hot enough where he has to have me.

I take him out of my mouth, his cock covered in my saliva, and say, "Baby?"

He doesn't look down. "Yes?"

"I want to feel your hands on me."

"Anything you want."

I stretch out on the sofa and he makes room for me as he comes up to kiss me. I love how he'll kiss me after I've sucked him. He's not shy or hung up about anything. He just wants me.

I wiggle out of my pants as Alan struggles with my blouse buttons. Soon, I'm naked and exposed to his strong hands.

Kissing me, he runs his hands over my breasts and belly. I grab a hand with my own and force it between my legs.

"Impatient, are we?"

I hum and groan and arch my hips into his hand. "Go easy. Gentle," I say. He runs the backs of his fingers up the length of my pussy. "Yes. Like that, baby."

As he kisses my mouth, his fingers slowly open my lower lips and run across the tip of my clit. My moan makes him speed up the assault on my clit. I break our kiss to whisper, "Easy."

He slows but keeps his focus on my firming nub. "Circle it with your finger."

Alan gets a rhythm going that includes dipping his fingers into my building wetness and bringing it up to make me wet from tip to tail. The wetter I get, the harder he works my clit and it's perfect.

"God. Put your fingers in me."

He wraps his arm around my shoulders to hold me tightly and forces two fingers into me. I arch and groan as he looks me in the eyes. He curves his fingers up to massage my G-spot and pumps harder.

"What do you want, baby?" Alan asks. "What can I do?"

"Take me to the bedroom."

Alan helps me up and leads the way to the bedroom. He

flicks off the light, but I switch it back on. "I want you to see."

I stretch out in the middle of the bed and pull Alan down on top of me. His delicious cock presses against my hip and I'm tempted to just fuck him. But there is something that has to be gotten past. I stop his fervent kisses long enough to say, "Lick me. Lick my pussy."

I'm so heated from his fingers. I put my hand on the top of his head and press him downward between my spread legs. Alan puts my legs over his shoulders.

"No, baby," I purr. "They've got to be flat on the bed. I tighten them up and the straighter the better." I widen my legs even farther to accommodate his wide shoulders.

His fingers make contact with my pussy and begin exploring, in and out of folds, around my clit and down. He's taking it slowly like we started on the sofa. I shut my eyes and take it in.

He spreads my lips and brings his mouth down to my clit, warm and wet.

"Massage it with your tongue, not flicking so much."

He does and I'm thrilled.

"Now, put your fingers in me and fuck me with them."

And he does.

I writhe under his mouth. It all feels so good. But good isn't going to be enough this time. This time I'm going to see colors.

"Harder, baby." I spread my fingers out on his head and press him into me.

I feel my orgasm growing in my muscles. My legs twitch and tighten. I want to bury my hands in his hair and push him into me. But I've done that before and all it does is make him not able to breathe. That's no good. Instead I grip his arm draped over my thigh, and the bedsheets—a big handful of bedsheets.

He slows his finger-fucking to concentrate on my clit. But I'm greedy.

"Put three fingers in and fuck me." *Oh, god, that's it!* "Now suck a little on my clit."

The pressure in my muscles, in my pussy, grows to a monumental level. I tighten and flex my legs. I lift my hips. I see the hurdle in front of us and I'm ready to jump.

I'm moaning and growling. I'm uttering obscenities. "God, baby! That's it! There! Yes!" With that, Alan pumps his hand harder and sticks with the sucking massage of my clit.

I squeeze my eyes shut, bear down and jump.

SEEING STARS

Louisa Harte

Tramping in New Zealand sounded great in the guidebook. *Follow well-worn trails through untouched wilderness*, it had said. It got the wilderness right. Two days into our five-day hike and already my legs are aching, I'm covered in bites and this damn tent is claustrophobic.

Of course, it had all been your idea. "C'mon, Zoe, it'll be fun," you'd coaxed. Lulled by a false sense of security at our luxury motel, I'd given in to your plea. Now here I am, one o'clock in the morning, wide awake, unable to sleep, and I'm seriously debating that decision.

There's no sympathy from you. I gaze over at you, cocooned in your sleeping bag beside me. You're fast asleep, like nothing can disturb you. Yet despite myself, I smile. This trip has shown me a new side of you. Not only does your brawny body look hot in tight shorts and boots, you look kind of sexy with a hint of stubble and mussed-up hair. And you're in your element with this self-sufficient lifestyle. On our daily hikes you've been giving

it your all, a goofy smile on your face as you lug that huge ruck-
sack on your back, taking my hand and guiding me through
long sodden grass and up steep hilly tracks, acting like a real
macho man. You've been all energy, fire and excitement. Until
you hit the sack. Then you're out like a light.

Typical.

Wrestling with the zip on my sleeping bag, I decide I need
some fresh air. I open the tent flap and peer outside. The day's
drizzle has cleared. Stars blink in the sky. The moon casts a pale
glow over the campsite, making it look strangely enticing. I tug
on my boots and pull on a light jacket over my pajamas. I'm
going out to explore.

Flicking on my flashlight, I step outside. I stand still for a
moment, letting my eyes adjust to the darkness. We've pitched
our tent at a remote spot by a lake. There are a few other tents
dotted about, but apart from that we're alone.

I wander over the grass, my boots squelching on the slippery
ground. A breeze ruffles my hair, blowing straight through the
flimsy material of my pajamas to prick at my skin. I shiver. It's
cool, but not unpleasant—more like exhilarating.

I find the track and head down to the lake. Something brushes
against my cheek. My mind fills with images of possums and
rats scampering toward me, and I swipe at the imaginary crit-
ters. Then I shine my flashlight to examine my assailant—it's just
a branch. I shake my head, realizing I'm being ridiculous. Thank
god you can't see me. I need to get a grip. This camping lark sure
takes some getting used to.

Stumbling on over the track, I hear an owl screech in the
trees. I stop and listen, becoming alert to the sounds around me.
Keeping still, I hear the hum of crickets and the gentle splash of
waves against the lakeshore. Then I hear something else. Something more guttural.

A moan.

I stop and gaze around. To my left there's a faint flicker of light coming from within one of the tents. Instinctively, I move closer. I switch off my light and strain for a closer look. In the dimness, I can faintly make out two figures. Writhing and moaning within their canvas enclosure, it's obvious they're fucking.

Suddenly the night takes on a new air. There's something raw and primal about it, something wanton. In the darkness, my senses are heightened. I shiver. It's thrilling.

Driven on by some inner urge, I move away from their tent and wander deeper into the bush. I seek out a quiet spot away from the path and sit down. I shrug off my jacket and lie back on the wet grass. No longer squeamish, I kick off my boots and dig my feet into the ground, enjoying the feeling of the damp earth between my toes. I close my eyes and breathe in the seductive scent of blossom as it carries on the breeze. I giggle, a kind of nervous, excited laugh that feels refreshing and unfamiliar. I feel different out here. Alive.

As I lie on the grass, savoring the scent of the woods and the sounds of the night, a strange unbidden thought goes through my head: *Why not indulge in a little pleasure of my own?* My eyes flick open, my mind battling with conflicting thoughts. *I can't—not here, surely?* a prim voice in my head scolds. *Why not?* another voice challenges.

My heart starts to thud against my chest. My body flushes and my mouth becomes dry at the thought. It's too delicious to resist. And hey—at least it will give me something to smile about as we scramble through more endless bush tomorrow.

Spurred on by this burst of kinky logic, I stretch out on the wet grass, preparing for ecstasy. As if playing along, the breeze picks up, tugging hard at my flimsy pajamas. Encouraged, I peel open my pajama top, button by button, letting the fabric fall open. The cool air brushes over my tits, making my nipples hard and tight. My skin tingles with anticipation as this invisible force plays with my body. I squirm against the grass, feeling heat and excitement begin to burn in my pussy. Closing my eyes, I search my mind for a raunchy fantasy to get myself started.

But I don't want one. Not tonight. Tonight I want something different—I want to be alive in the moment.

I flick open my eyes and tune in to the energy of the environment, feeding off its earthy vibes. A smile on my lips, I hunker down in the grass and slide my hand into my pajama pants to play with my pussy. I gasp, surprised at my wetness. Swirling my fingers in my juice, I coat each one before stroking my slit. My clit strains, hard and eager for attention. I graze it with my thumb. Stroke it. Tease it a little. I love playing with myself, building that familiar ache until it becomes an overwhelming desire that takes over my body. I've always loved wanking, being the one in control, timing my pleasure to perfection. Only tonight I have a surprise participant—nature. Goose bumps prickle my skin as the wind gusts over my bare tits. It lifts my hair and throws it across my face like a kinky blindfold. I moan with pleasure and wiggle my hips, shoving my ass deeper into the sodden grass in response.

Moving my hand lower, I dip a finger into my cunt. My cunt grasps at it, eager and hungry. I can't believe how horny I feel, how thrilling and lewd this is, playing outdoors. Moving my thumb back to my clit, I stroke it, circle it, rub it gently, then harder.

My arousal builds. Pleasure flutters low in my belly, tightening muscles and taking my breath. The wind rattles the tree above me, sending leaves scattering over my naked body. I sigh. I arch my back and offer myself up to the elements. I'm blending into the outdoors, becoming part of it—relishing its pure unadulterated eroticism.

The wind picks up. Clouds gather above and raindrops begin

to fall. I hear them patter in the leaves above. A drop splashes my face and slides down my cheek. I smile and open my mouth, letting the fresh, cool liquid coat my tongue. It's delicious. The experience feels organic—primal.

I can't get enough of it.

I shiver as rain splashes my tits and soaks my pajamas, yet the wetter I get, the more turned on I become. I tune in to my body, trying to note every movement and shudder. I want to savor it all so that I can reflect on it later—add this experience to my ever-growing collection of fantasies.

Then my thoughts drift to you, asleep in the tent, while I'm out here, fucking myself on the damp grass. I'm so near and yet so far away; it's like I'm in another place, another world. And I love it. I whimper and writhe shamelessly against my hand—free in the darkness to become someone else, someone reckless and abandoned.

I feel the first tremors of orgasm flicker inside me. My heart beats faster. It pulses in my chest and throbs in my crotch, urging me to finish the deed.

I rub my finger over my clit. Faster. Harder. My cheeks flush, my eyelashes flutter. I'm close. So close. My legs tense and I grit my teeth, preparing for the explosion I know is coming...

...Oh, and it comes all right.

I hold my hand still as delicious spasms pulse through my pussy, spilling pleasure through my body. I moan and buck my hips, tossing my head from side to side, letting the full, raw power of my orgasm rock my body and blister my mind.

It takes a few moments to come down from my climax. Slowly, my muscles relax and my breathing settles. I smile and spread myself out over the wet grass like it's a luxurious bed.

And then I hear something: a rustle in the trees. Someone is out here.

I lift my head. A flashlight beam sweeps the path beside me. I freeze: hold my breath and shrink down, trying to disappear. The beam gets closer. It's like something out of a film. And just like a character in a film, I'm too shocked and scared to move a muscle.

The beam of light moves away from the path and starts to scan over the grass toward me. I swallow as it settles on my discarded boots, watch wide-eyed as it gets closer and closer. I gasp as the beam pans over my seminaked body. Then I squint against the bright light as the beam hits my face.

The light wavers. Then I hear a voice, breathless. "Zoe?"

Scrabbling in the grass beside me, I make a grab for my flashlight and shine it up at my accuser.

My heart leaps into my throat. *It's you.*

We train our lights on each other, like a duel in the dark. I wonder who will make the first move.

You do. You gaze down at me, taking in my flushed cheeks and my bared breasts. I watch as your expression changes from concern to interest, then lust. "I wondered where you'd got to." Your voice is strained, husky.

"I was just…" I search for an excuse. But there are none. The truth's written all over my face. Even thinking about it gets me all hot and wet again. "…Exploring…" I add feebly.

Your brows lift. Your gaze lowers to my hand still tucked down my pants. "I can see that," you murmur.

I wonder if you're joking, if you're angry or upset. But then I notice your cock pitching its own tent in your boxers and I smirk. "Well, you did say we should be self-sufficient…"

Your lips twitch. A smile? You meet my gaze and see the gleam in my eyes, reflecting a new, different side of me, wild and abandoned. "Self-sufficiency's overrated," you whisper. You flick off your flashlight and drop to your knees in front of me. Stroking your hand over my breasts, you prize the flashlight from my hand.

And switch it off.

Plunged back into darkness, I feel my pajama pants slide down over my hips to my ankles. I swallow. Now I have another participant—you. Tugging off my pajamas, you toss them aside and push open my legs. I feel your warm breath on my thighs as you inch your way slowly up toward my crotch. The first orgasm was great, but the prospect of another almost has me begging, and I thrust my hips up to meet you. You chuckle and grab my ass in your big rough hands. There's a delicious pause, then you plunge your face into my pussy.

I groan. I clutch your shoulders and writhe against you as your tongue spears my cunt. The wind lifts your thick hair, spreading it over my pussy like a blanket. I squeal in delight as it tickles my skin. At the mercy of the wind's teasing caress and your tongue's expert probing, I squirm shamelessly, enjoying this delightful threesome between me, you and nature.

Rain continues to fall. The cold splash of raindrops over my tits contrasts with the heat of your lips on my slit. I rock my hips in your face as you flick your tongue at my clit, encouraging you. You swirl your tongue over my bud before covering it with your mouth. Spreading my legs wider, I moan in approval. You nibble and suck like a pro—"going bush" in the rawest sense of the term. Pleasure builds inside me and I take a deep breath, feeling the orgasm grow in my belly.

Obligingly, you lave me harder. I curl my fingers in your hair and tense my legs as the climax takes hold.

I cry out. My legs shake, my hips buck and suddenly I'm flooded with sensations: the wind, the rain, you and these delicious contractions, all converging in one huge, great orgasm. Grasping my thighs, you hold me tight, riding out the convulsions with me.

Gradually, the tremors subside. In the darkness I can sense

you smiling, enjoying my pleasure as if it's your own. You always were a thoughtful lover.

A shaft of moonlight shines through a break in the clouds, illuminating us. You lift your head from between my thighs, a mischievous look on your face. "So, are you enjoying this trip now?" you murmur.

I prop myself up on my elbows to look at you. A cheeky smile crosses my lips and I nod.

I guess being intimate with nature *does* have its perks.

OLD FAITHFUL

Sylvia Lowry

I received the postcard from Clive and Margaret and hid it scorn-fully in the bookcase between the 1958 and 1959 *World Alma-nacs*. There was some poetic truth in leaving the previous year's edition coupled on the shelf with the new; I imagined myself mired in time, hopelessly static and imprisoned in the previous year, and the contents of the postcard had only darkened my mood. Clive's cloying tone and cheerful double entendre had opened latent wounds, and his words were expressed with the inane self-seeking chatter of the honeymooner: *We have seen little of Yellowstone, of course, and are relishing our view of the knotty pine walls of our hotel room.* The opposite side displayed a photo of Old Faithful; I imagined Clive's semen spurting grace-lessly all over Margaret's backside.

My own morning was far from orgasmic and the same could be said for my married life, a veritable carnal dust bowl, my soli-tude heightened by the blare of "Kookie, Kookie, Lend Me Your Comb" on the radio, and the inane, insistent chirp of birds in

the vacant avenue outside. The tail fin of every passing Cadillac
or DeSoto reminded me of an erect cock, poised to deliver the
gratification that I was terminally denied. My husband was in
Manhattan, expending his sexual reserves on empty careerism
and perhaps another woman. I knew that the cliché was utterly
rote, and the reflection inspired to me to laugh as I smoked a
second cigarette, watching Ernie Kovacs unfurl in dismal gray
lines on the television and caressing the folds of my housecoat. I
savored the irony of the garment's design; it had all the trappings
of the apparel of seduction, elegant and teasingly transparent,
remaining destined for an empty audience of pans, dishrags and
Borax bleach. Mine was lacy black, perfect attire for Bluebeard's
prisoner or a ward of the seraglio.

I reclined on the couch and felt a hard object beneath me. It
was a toy robot, abandoned by my nephew John the previous
week, and I idly turned its key and watched it sputter across
the floor, whirring and shaking wildly, eyes sparkling capri-
ciously. There is something about contemplating the objects of
childhood when you're in a less-than-innocent mood; there is
first a maudlin craving for the ease and purity of early days, a
cheerful simplicity that leads to more wicked adult impulses with
distressing ease. I picked up the toy, which continued to vibrate in
my hand, stroking its round metal head as "The Happy Organ"
shuddered through the radio in an anxious discharge of sound.
I lay back on the couch, turning the key as I thrust my panties
downward, first leaving them stranded at my thighs then casting
them toward the hi-fi, nearly striking the jacket of a Chet Baker
album. The jazzman stared back at me, fragile and melancholic,
the sole witness to my upcoming act of subversion.

I innocently kissed the robot's head in a brief tribute before
I applied the quivering headpiece to my clit, first recoiling
from the violence of the metallic surface before pressing more

emphatically then leaning backward, feeling a delicious sensation emerge, pinching my swelling nipples as I found myself blowing a dirty kiss to the observing face of Chet, muttering "Fuck, fuck, fuck," as if my desperate mantra could conjure a lover from the empty, sweltering air. I briefly envisioned Robbie the Robot as a cock of flesh; I pushed the head inside as my pussy grew wetter, feeling the slick rounded surface caress my labia as it continued its quivering journey inward, finally wanting to weep at the tragic incompleteness of my orgasm as the toy reached an inevitable impasse. Too broad to allow deeper entry, the shuddering steel floundered at the heavenly gates, arms and legs writhing as its delicious head plumbed my anointed cunt. I exhaled dramatically, surrendering to the compromised, metallic half-fuck, caressing my clit in a circular motion before slapping it feverishly, sensing a partial sensation of release rising from my vulva and via a mischievous conduit through my nipples and throat. I gazed toward Chet, silently imploring his aid as I abandoned my experiment, dropping the robot to the floor, where its febrile motion slowed, and it lay prone and abject, discarded like an incompetent lover. My climax remained incomplete.

Perspiring, I wiped my face, opening my housecoat as I wandered into the basement. Still filled with my morning laundry, the ringer washer vibrated in darkness, green against black, water cascading violently against its interior, a pure carnal force shuddering viscerally in the blackness. I embraced it, imagining myself joining a mechanical lover of sublime magnitude, grinding my naked pussy into the pulsating steel curvature of the tank, a giant tremulous cock fucking me into oblivion. Its attentions triggered an immediate response, and I sensed the reemergence of my thwarted orgasm as I propelled my cunt inward; the trembling steel caressed my clit and entire pussy in a single, awe-inspiring motion. I eased my tits into the embrace, allowing my nipples to achieve intimate contact with the rigid steel, feeling an initial shock of cold quickly transfigured into an inverse sensation of scorching heat, a miasma of conflicting impressions that impelled me to gaze skyward, muttering, "Fuck me, fuck me, fuck me," in an attempt to animate the iron beast into pliant flesh.

But as the climactic moment approached, I heard the doorbell ring and recoiled backward from the washer, cursing my impulsive reaction; it reminded me of my engrained servitude. A force of habit more powerful than my fading animal urges had impelled me to button up my housecoat and revert to my role as acquiescent, neutered domestic angel. I swore as I climbed the stairs, bliss fading as I ascended into the heat of the upper floors.

Opening the door, I saw a young man standing on the threshold, holding a single vacuum cleaner, his jacket suspended across his arm, wiping perspiration from his forehead in a studied, dramatic gesture. In the glare of the sun, now intense and prismatic, he almost looked like Chet Baker, hair slicked backward, mildly dispassionate and introverted, somehow mired in an impossible task. Or so I imagined; my fading arousal, the overwhelming heat, and the forces of isolation had conspired against my rational thoughts, which I imagined melting into oblivion, dispersed onto the pavement.

"Ma'am, can I impose on you for a glass of water?" He looked downward, which seemed to confirm the modest candor of the request.

"Of course." I opened the door, smiling ritually as I gestured for him to enter. "But you won't escape the heat inside. I'll reward you by letting you make your sales pitch in reasonable comfort."

He raised his eyebrows. "You sound so cynical. Are you certain there is a sales pitch?"

I laughed, I hoped benevolently, gently seeking forgiveness

for my sarcasm. "Honey, I'm here all day. I get caught up in the rhythms of commerce all the time." I retreated to the kitchen and poured a glass of water, which he drank with indelicate speed as I watched from a distance. He set the glass down and straightened his tie. I unbuttoned my housecoat in counterpoint.

"I've been to four houses on the block. No one wants to buy."

I frowned playfully. "Maybe no one appreciates technology. I know Ms. Adams next door still loves her broom. Personally, I like machines—they break the solitude somehow."

"I don't understand."

I wandered the room, feeling a lyrical melancholy counterpoised against a new arousal. "I'm all alone in time and space, young man. My husband could just as well be on Mars. My so-called friends are fucking their brains out in Yellowstone. Lucky motherfuckers." I laughed as he started, eyes twitching in incredulity at my indecency. "I apologize for my indelicate speech…a little."

He paused, regaining his composure. "Ma'am, maybe you'd like me to demonstrate…" He reached toward the vacuum. It languished in the sun: long, metallic, another ominous implement of pleasure.

"Wait." I lit a cigarette and blew a cloud into the air, imaging the force of my thoughts crossing the room as diffused smoke, asserting their impious influence. "Let me make you a pitch instead."

"What?" He paused, browbeaten. He trembled as if his practiced speech and routine had been utterly disrupted.

"First loosen your tie." I crossed my legs and took another drag on the cigarette, smiling through one corner of my mouth as he released his top button and relaxed the grip of the tie on his neck. In the corner of my vision, I could see the Chet Baker LP and could envision the jazzman nodding in unity,

whispering, "Every Cloud Has a Silver Lining" as the tie dropped
to the floor. It lay sad and desultory on the carpet, a symbol of
discarded propriety.

"And your pitch?" He looked toward me, awaiting further
instruction.

"Take off your pants." He fumbled in the act but obeyed
readily, charmingly folding the apparel as if his sales pretensions
remained intact. I unbuttoned my housecoat farther, revealing
my tits as I walked forward and caressed the outline of his cock
through his briefs, sensing a rising, startled tumescence; I capri-
ciously played with the head, now swelling in response to my
touch. "Now." I looked him in the eyes, summoning my reserves
of command. "I want you to stick this"—I squeezed his cock affec-
tionately—"into your lovely machine. And I want to watch…"

He swallowed visibly. "But how?" The desperate thought
trailed into oblivion.

"How is it gonna get hard enough? Here, honey." I seized
his waistband and pulled his briefs down in a single rapid
gesture, licking his shaft as I murmured an inarticulate encour-
agement, caressing each ardent, pulsing vein with my tongue as
if I were savoring a fine wine, wondering how long it had been
since I had tasted a cock. Finally sensing the shaft achieving
full rigidity, I salivated charitably as I sucked the head, kissing
it in gentle homage as I grasped the base and jacked him off
with one hand. I fully discarded my housecoat; the crumpled
garment lingered on the carpet like a black hole on a pristine
field, negating time and space. I imagined myself spitting on it,
a final gesture of liberation as I drooled on his cock, placing the
shaft between my breasts as I caressed his erection with the pure
enveloping friction of my décolletage, sensing a rising ardor as
I prepared my next command.

"Turn on the vacuum and stick your fucking cock in."

"But..."

I laughed with a note of impatience. "Just fucking do it." I sat back on the couch, appetizingly naked and exposed, reigniting my cigarette as the machine roared to life. I imagined a rocket jettisoning off to Pluto, or perhaps some reptilian, carnal quadrant of my brain. He placed his erect cock in the open aperture of the vacuum, which received it graciously and fervently; lost to its infernal suction, he began to chant, "Oh, fuck, oh, fuck, oh, fuck," as the force drew him inward.

And as I watched him writhe in elation, I began to play with my pussy and clit, its sodden arousal returning, enamored by the spectacle before me, banishing solitude and anguish, surrendering to a rising crescendo, placing first one and then a second finger inside myself, imagining the pliant salesman as my absent husband, damned to be my docile plaything, ensnared by my filthy commands. Wordlessly, the vacuum roared its carnal music of the spheres as I stood and grabbed the salesman's head and seized his oily locks of hair, compelling his face into my pussy. He began to lick, first tentatively and with slobbering indirection, then with greater vigor as his tongue plumbed my cunt, progressing with subservient logic to my clit, where it remained, lapping with anxious fervor. As my latent orgasm began to rise, inspiring a potent frisson across my vulva, I released his head, casting him backward as I turned off the vacuum, leaning back onto the couch and spreading my pussy in invitation, twisting my nipples with my other hand. I blew a naughty kiss in his direction, but he was anxiously surveying his cock, still erect and liberated from the declining force of the machine.

I drew idly on my cigarette and whispered, "Come here and let me wrap my pussy around that fucking cock." He looked upward, as if the thought were entangled in his battered consciousness, compelling me to grab the base of the flagging member, jacking it off as I pulled it toward me. A Studebaker, tail fins resplendent, soared past the window, a rocket caressing the ether. He plunged into me at the same moment, the force of his entry knocking me farther into the couch, as if the nose cone of a missile, propelled with the force of a moon shot, had thrust its breadth inside me. I clutched the pillows as he began a fusillade of strokes while I lurched forward, grunting like a beast, biting his neck impulsively as the strokes continued with a fatalistic intensity, as if he would sacrifice his life for the fleeting joys of an animated fuck.

And perhaps I would have, too, knowing that bliss can only be fleeting and is doomed to perish at its height. Chet smiled from a distance and the ineffable sound of a cymbal shuddered across my brain as he continued to fuck me, slapping my clit to hasten the arrival of the deferred climax. He briefly paused, the shaft shuddering before he resumed his efforts while I caressed his balls, imagining a torrent of come percolating, poised to erupt from his tightening scrotum, safely cradled in my calculating grasp. He slowed, perspiring, pushing his cock into my cunt more deeply, as if to compensate for his reduced pace, triggering a concentrated sensation that detonated through my pussy and toward my tonsils; I could feel my crotch dripping, dousing his cock with amplified moisture as a new impression rose from the depths of my pussy, shuddering like frenzied clockwork, expanding as an ineffable undercurrent. The sensation rose through my nipples and tendons, as if my senses were united by a single conduit, and then I sensed a seismic convulsion. My abdomen and ass shook, as if I had incarnated an earthquake, the upheaval continuing as I announced, "Keep fucking me," half animal utterance and half command.

The vacuum remained within my grasp, and I reached down to seize the nozzle and flip the switch, applying its infernal suction to my clit as he fucked harder, lurching into me like a brute. I could feel my pussy rise, standing at attention, caressed by steel, drenched and exhilarated. And as if my tremors had released it from the shelf, I could see that Clive's postcard had fallen to the floor, his inane handwriting mercifully facing the carpet. The froth of Old Faithful lurched upward, and I concentrated on the ascending spray as I plumbed my tongue into the salesman's ear, relishing the propulsive motion of his cock, each stroke adding incremental friction, tickling my clit with the margins of the steel tube, inspiring my tremor to rise. I clenched my teeth and suppressed the impulse to devour the poor bastard's earlobe. I imagined myself lurching into a cannibal frenzy as I propelled my hips forward to complement his thrusts, my consciousness retreating into prehistoric longing, away from rockets and tail fins and hi-fis and into a primordial miasma of pure fucking and ecstatic sensation, screaming like a Cro-Magnon as he withdrew, coming in a round of rapid explosions, the bursts of semen striking my pussy as I unleashed a fountain of my own. As if a floodgate had opened, a cataract of fluid erupted from my pussy as I ejaculated onto his cock. The twin streams of my juice and his come merged, an elemental fusion of two essences, twin forces of nature in synergy, or perhaps something more cosmic: I imagined a missile traveling a graceful arc of emancipation. The vacuum groaned, half purring, vibrating like a skyrocket.

I ran my hand through the sticky mixture, murmuring and lapping greedily as I kissed my palm, tasting something ineffable—the taste of a euphoric fuck distilled into a single, transitory flavor. I collapsed backward, and I could see the postcard again, the spume of Old Faithful bearing witness to my pleasure. The robot came back to life and writhed on the floor, as if a spasm of pleasure had seized its iron frame.

PAYING IT FORWARD

Kendra Wayne

Dear Pamela,

Thank you, thank you, a thousand times thank you!

Jayne (& Simon)

The card was cream colored, heavy stock, the front bearing a swirl of doves with ribbons in their beaks. A photo had slipped out when she'd opened the envelope: the happy couple, toasting.

Pamela hadn't been invited to the wedding (that would have been awkward and inappropriate). She hadn't, technically, sent a gift (at least, not to celebrate the nuptials). But she was truly touched that the bride (whom she'd never met) had taken the time to express her gratitude.

She tapped the card thoughtfully against her lower lip. Which one had Simon been? She pondered the picture again. He definitely looked familiar. She judged him to be about thirty, which meant she'd known him less than ten years ago. She never chose someone younger than twenty-three; that was her rule.

She poured herself a glass of tawny port, pulled out a flowered hatbox—unusually romantic storage that would surprise anyone who knew her—and settled on the sofa. She kept no photos of those she tutored, only a single souvenir from each to jog her memory. Now she sifted through them: a playing card (the queen of spades), a plastic purple dinosaur (the cereal-prize kind), an unsigned bookplate, a leopard-print satin mask, a half-melted green candle, a postcard of a winter landscape.

The guitar pick had slipped toward the bottom of the box. She turned it over in her fingers. Ah, *Simon.* Now she remembered him.

He'd been shyer than most, emboldened more by her friendliness than alcohol. He'd also been her last that year. She could only do so much, teach so many, in a season.

Simon, with his black hair a little too long and falling into his eyes: he was in a band. Not her usual type—her standard operating procedure was to pick out a grad student; law, maybe, or an MBA candidate. Occasionally she chose a medical intern, but they were hard to find, generally too busy and too tired and too distracted.

Simon played bass, and he played it with a concentrated ferocity that hinted at his offstage self. He focused on the instrument, not on the crowd. He didn't have that indefinable stage presence, and some women found that fascinating. But Pamela also noticed he was a little shy, that he often missed their overtures. Not rude, not snubbing, just...oblivious.

She'd talked to him, drawn him out, waiting until the bar was nearly empty each night and pouring herself a drink to mirror his. People tended to open up more when you did that,

she'd discovered. She always paid for her own drinks, adding
the money to the till. The bartending jobs didn't pay her bills;
they were a side venture, a way to meet young men like Simon.

The first time they'd fucked, she'd found he fucked like he
played bass. Intense, focused, but not entirely aware of the reaction he was receiving. He touched her in all the right places,
sucked and licked and fondled her, and yes, she'd come more
than once before he entered her.

But he'd paid attention from a distant place, as if pleasuring
her was a test he had to pass. He'd enjoyed it, but not fed off it,
not gained pleasure from her pleasure.

That was why he was a competent musician, not a brilliant
one. She'd realized right then she might just kill two birds with
one stone with him.

So she'd started teaching him. She slowed him down, showed
him how her body reacted to what he did. Eventually she'd tied
him up—light, fun bondage only, no need to scare the poor
boy—and made him more aware of his own body and how it
reacted.

To her delight, finally one night he came just from making
her come. He'd been eating her out, his fingers as talented inside
her as they were on his instrument (and the rough calluses didn't
hurt). She'd stiffened and cried out her pleasure, shuddering and
clamping down on him, and dimly she'd heard him groan. The
vibration of the sound on his lips had extended her orgasm.

When she came back to earth, she found he'd spurted on
the bedspread. His expression was a mixture of stunned lust
and embarrassment, and she'd assured him it wasn't a problem;
quite the opposite.

You've learned well, grasshopper. Time for your next lesson.

Not just the next lesson, but the whole point of her tutelage.
The reason she took them under her wing, year after year.

All the women's magazines purported to be open and free when it came to sexual advice, their covers promising that inside was The Secret to Ultimate Pleasure. (Often his, rather than hers, but that was a rant for another day.) They purported to have a positive, open attitude toward sex.

Then one day a reader had written in to ask about anal sex. And the magazine had lambasted the idea.

Disgusting, filthy, perverted, it announced (all of which seemed positive to Pamela). Besides, it was painful and dangerous, and no self-respecting woman would actually want to do it.

Well, yes, it could be painful when done wrong. But Pamela, as self-respecting as any woman, *did* enjoy it, a whole hell of a lot.

She did what she could to promote it as normal, healthy and even fun (although the magazine pointedly chose not to publish the letter she'd written as a rebuttal to the columnist), but that's when the second part of the problem cropped up.

Women might want it, but men didn't know how to do it to them.

Which started Pamela's crusade to teach them.

"I want to do something different tonight," she told Simon. They were showering together after one of his gigs, a perfect lead-in. "Something a little…naughty."

His grin was a mixture of excited and shy; his cock was just excited, twitching against her hip. "Sure. You haven't steered me wrong yet."

She put her lips to his ear, the water pounding around them. "Anal sex," she said and ran her fingernails lightly down his ass.

His cock throbbed again. "But we've already…"

Yes, she'd slipped a finger or two inside him, shown him how a massage against his prostate could make him come like a geyser.

"No," she said. "Me. I want your cock stuffed in my ass."

He had the perfect cock for it, too. Not too thick but with a nice, crowned head. Her ass had clenched in anticipation the first time she'd seen him naked.

Her words had the desired effect. Now he was rock hard beneath her soapy hand, and she used that to further advantage, inviting him to rub himself against her ass to get everything squeaky clean.

In the bedroom, she'd already laid out lube, pillows, a string of beads. Toweled off, she draped herself over the pillows, ass in the air. At her suggestion, he licked. He was tentative at first, but her moans of approval spurred him to greater boldness.

So good. God, yes. He pressed against her, the tip of his tongue pointed and just barely entering her—a tease, a promise of things to come.

"Feel how wet I am," she hissed.

"Damn, you are," he said, sounding surprised and pleased. He slipped his fingers between her lips and coated them with her juices. Then he painted her anus and licked her clean. She hadn't even had to ask. He was a quick learner, this callus-fingered bassist.

She smiled, told him to get the lube.

He was appropriately gentle, sliding one finger into her, then two, stretching her out a little.

"Now the beads," she said. Did she sound like she was begging? Maybe she was, just a little.

He greased them up, carefully slipped them in. She shivered, savoring the sensations, each little pop of pleasure ratcheting her arousal higher.

She rolled off the pillows onto her back and spread her legs. Simon knew what to do. Lips and tongue and fingers, tasting and teasing, flicking and sucking. He even tugged on the string, smart boy, and she clenched and released around the beads.

Thighs tensing, belly quivering, teetering on the edge, she moaned, "Pull them out."

As they eased out of her, one by excruciating one, she came.

Simon crawled up to kiss her, barely letting her catch her breath. "That was amazing," he said.

"Darling," she said when she was able, "that was just the appetizer." She sat up, leaned over to swipe her tongue across the precome that glistened on his cockhead. "You didn't think I'd forget you, did you?"

She pressed him back on the bed and coated her hands with lube, rubbing her palms together to warm up the slick gel before wrapping her fingers around his hard length. She oiled him up and straddled him.

He was so slippery, it was a challenge to keep him poised at the entrance to her ass. The anal beads were no match for his girth (slender and perfect as he was), but she finally got him trapped, the head of his cock partway in.

"The trick...is to go slow." It was hard to talk through the near-spasms of pleasure. She rocked up and down, letting just a little more of him in each time as she loosened up. "The first time or two, it's best to let the lady call the shots. Once you're familiar with each other, you can switch places...put her on her knees, on her back. Oh, fuck yes."

The head of his cock had popped in. All that was left was that first, delicious, slow sinking down on him, feeling him fill her most intimate spot.

"Holy shit," he gasped, and then barked a laugh, realizing what he'd said. She breathed out a chuckle.

"Nice and tight," she managed. "You like?" His answer was a groan of pure pleasure.

Anal sex was the one act that made her hair stand up. Strange way of putting it, but there you had it. It was as if her entire body was electrified, every cell on alert, tingling.

And an anal orgasm was like no other. Right now Simon was too far gone to help, his arms spread as if he were the one impaled in some unholy, exquisite rite. So she took matters into her own hands, stroking her fat clit, feeling it quiver beneath her fingers as she increased the pace of fucking him. The masturbation would help tip her over the edge, but the true pleasure was having his cock stuffed in her ass, stretching her, stroking her from the inside.

Next time she'd let him take the lead while she bent over the bed, fisting the sheets in her hands and begging incoherently.

The shuddering started deep in her spine. She felt his cock swell, stretching her further, and his orgasm was the final trigger she needed. His hips rose off the bed as she convulsed and came around him.

Ah, Simon. Pamela sighed, dropping the pick back into the box. He was one of her best, and she was pleased Jayne appreciated what she'd taught him.

She poured herself another glass of port and headed to the bedroom. She didn't normally indulge in reminiscence, but tonight she'd pull out her anal vibrator and some lube and toast the happy couple in the best way she knew how.

Then, tomorrow, it was time to go out and find her next student.

THE BIG O

Donna George Storey

W ho would have guessed that the circle would begin in the ladies' lounge at the Claremont spa? Yet there I was, sipping cucumber-infused water and leafing through women's magazines, when I happened upon a peppy two-page article that would change my life.

The Sexercise Prescription: A Stronger Secret You in Six Weeks.

At first the headline made me snicker, but then a deeper stirring—call it a presentiment of destiny—made me fold back the page and begin to read. Of course, I'd heard of Kegel exercises before. I'd even tried them once or twice. I never kept it up though, because it always struck me as somehow perverted to exercise my muscles *down there*. That was for strippers, chicks that had to pick up twenty-dollar bills with their pussies, not ordinary market research analysts like me.

Of course, my life had been anything but ordinary since I met Adam last January at a coworker's wedding. I'd never known a man who was as unfailingly kind, funny and considerate of all my needs. The sex alone was so shatteringly transcendental, I felt like I had to glue my body parts back together afterward. Over the months I'd come to appreciate the serenity of a boyfriend who slipped out of bed at dawn to meditate for an hour every morning and relaxed after a hard day teaching high school history by drawing O shapes with a Japanese brush and glossy black ink.

There was just one drawback. Adam's idea of the perfect summer vacation was to fly to Kyoto to sit *zazen* for a month. As you might guess, we didn't exactly find common ground there.

I was still pretty mad about it the night before he left. Even when Adam tried to make love to me, I just lay there, sullen and passive. He was depriving me of pleasure for so long, why shouldn't he get a taste of his own medicine? I should have known I'd lose my resolve to Adam's soft tongue circling my nipples, his fingers patiently coaxing my clit to full attention. It felt so good when he was eating my pussy, I decided to come on his face to spite him, but he pulled away at the very last minute, leaving me begging him for more. He took me close to the summit, then backed away twice more before he finally let me come around his cock. The orgasm practically blew my head off.

After that, I wasn't mad anymore, but I did wonder how I was going to survive without that transcendent pleasure.

That was one reason why the headline drew my attention. It just so happened Adam would be in Japan for six weeks, travel included. For most of that time he'd be completely out of touch—no phone, no Internet. That left a lot of time to fill with spa facials, outings with my friends, and now, perhaps a naughty new strengthening routine. The article promised if I did three simple exercises every day, I'd notice a definite improvement in my PC muscle tone and the intensity of my orgasms in forty-two days. My fortunate lover, the author added coyly, would be delighted with my new skills, too.

I bit my lip and pondered the path before me. Finding this article the day after Adam left seemed like karma, although Adam would argue that word merely meant cause-and-effect and not a sign from the Universe.

At that very moment, the other spa guest reading *Glamour* on the chair across from me was called away for her massage, leaving me alone in the room. I decided the Universe was definitely speaking. I quickly tore the article from the magazine and slipped it in the pocket of my robe.

If everything went as advertised, Adam might well find the path to nirvana *after* he got home.

I was anxious to get started with the program, but the article suggested I choose a private, comfortable place and take my time for the first sessions. Once I got the basics down, I could supposedly do my Kegels while driving or sitting in boring meetings at work. That night, after dinner out with a friend, I got ready for bed early and lit the candle on the nightstand for extra atmosphere. Adam and I liked making love by candlelight, and as I stretched out on my side of the futon, I felt a sudden pang of longing for his warmth, his knowing fingers stroking me in my tender places. I closed my eyes and took a deep breath. To my surprise, the loneliness immediately dissolved into a reassuring glow in my belly.

Still breathing mindfully, I made a mental rundown of the "sexercises." First I was supposed to tighten my PC muscle, hold for a count of ten, then exhale slowly. On my next breath, I dutifully squeezed my secret muscles, trying my best not to tense other parts of my body. The tightness in my groin felt odd, as if I had a full bladder, but when I relaxed, the urgent feeling faded back into a soothing glow. I was still a little worried. What if I was so out of shape down there, six weeks wouldn't be enough for Adam to notice a change?

This was no place for perfectionism, I reminded myself. As Adam always said, a journey of a thousand miles begins with one step—or maybe one squeeze?

The next exercise was a series of twenty quick contractions, like a butterfly fluttering its wings. Again I felt clumsy. There was no teacher to turn to for help like I had in my yoga class. By the end, though, the tingling between my legs told me my muscles had gotten a good workout.

But I still had the biggest hurdle ahead—"the elevator." The article said I was supposed to contract my vagina in three stages: the outer lips first, then the middle section, and finally the deepest muscles near my cervix. After holding for a count of five, the elevator returned to home base with the release of each "floor."

As I reread the instructions, I realized I was blushing. Lying here in bed in my nightshirt, my pelvis tilted up and my legs parted, it struck me how shamelessly sensual this "inner-strength" routine was after all. I was in fact *training* my pussy for sex. But I was a nice girl, and nice girls weren't supposed to devote themselves to the study of amorous techniques so they could milk their boyfriends' dicks like vacuum cleaners as a welcome-home present.

Of course, nice girls weren't known for having much fun, either.

Pursing my lips in concentration, I tentatively tightened my opening. So far, so good; the elevator door was closed and ready to climb to the first floor. I squeezed higher. To my surprise, I actually did feel a band of muscle contract a few inches deeper in my pelvis. The last stop was more elusive, just a faint twinge up near my belly button. But I was so relieved I'd managed to feel something, my "elevator" plummeted to the ground floor in one quick exhalation. Still, I gamely pulled my "elevator" up and down ten times in all.

When I was done, I was not only feeling a real buzz between my legs, my panties were noticeably damp. Even my breasts felt swollen and aching to be touched. Now I understood why the author suggested practicing in a private place. The exercises definitely got you in the mood, and it would be a lot harder to finish things right in the car or a conference room.

Here in bed, though, I was free to shimmy out of my underwear and burrow my middle finger between my pussy lips without so much as a "Mind if I masturbate while you give your presentation, Boss?"

My clit felt especially hard tonight, a rigid pearl slipping around under the slick, satiny skin of my vulva. To my surprise, my pussy muscles contracted again, involuntarily, sending a wave of pleasure crashing up my spine.

What would happen if I did the exercises while I played with myself? I strummed faster and squeezed. The sensation was definitely more intense. I pumped my muscle again, thinking of Adam and his yummy dick. In fact my pussy did feel like a hungry mouth, famished for a hard cock, but grasping only air.

Form is emptiness; emptiness is form.

Adam's deep voice filled my head, as if he were right beside me on the futon. Suddenly in my mind's eye I did see him, sitting with his knees tucked beneath him, holding the brush he used to draw the *ensô*, the circle that is both nothing and everything.

Open your legs, Maddy.

His voice was kind, but commanding.

I dropped my thighs open for him.

Press your lips open, so I can see your hole.

With a sigh, I pushed out for him.

Without another word, he slipped the tip of the brush inside me. I gasped. Did he mean to push it in all the way and fuck me with it? I was horny enough to like the idea. But instead, he made a few quick back-and-forth motions, as he did when he inked his brush, then withdrew.

I groaned in disappointment.

Open as wide as you can now, Maddy.

His tone was so reassuring, I obediently pushed my "elevator door" open. Murmuring approval, Adam rested the brush just to the side of my clit and began to trace my inner lips in one smooth, practiced motion.

The way he did when he drew the circle of emptiness.

Emptiness.

In fact, I had always thought of my vagina as an empty hole, a negative space to be filled. But the sensation of his slippery brush seemed to awaken a presence, the dormant power in the flesh itself. I could feel the tender skin growing fat and full and strong beneath his touch. But then Adam paused, maddeningly, right before he reached my throbbing clit.

I cried out in frustration, but in the next instant I was coming anyway, my orgasm jerking my body on the bed like an earthquake. With all the howling and thumping, I'm surprised the neighbors didn't call the police.

Afterward, I smoothed the crumpled pages of the magazine and laid them carefully on my nightstand for future reference.

These next six weeks on my own might not be so bad after all.

I wouldn't exactly call it an addiction. Let's just say the Sexercise Prescription was one workout routine I had no trouble fitting into my busy schedule. In fact, as suggested, I did the official three-part series on my way to work and even squeezed in a few during boring meetings. But I always waited until I got home to do the fourth part of the series.

After a few weeks, I'd settled into a very pleasurable routine. First I stripped naked and knelt in the middle of the futon. After I warmed myself up with a set of exercises, I'd close my eyes and take a deep breath.

Suddenly, I'm no longer alone in my bedroom.

Instead I'm in a mirrored dance studio, with a dozen students kneeling in a circle around me, all eager to become strong inside just like me. They are all nude, too, and I take a moment to admire their beauty. Some have enviably curvy figures—lush hips and full bosoms that beg to be weighed in my hands. Others are boyish with high, tight buttocks and perky breasts. The diversity of grooming habits catches my attention, too. A few wax themselves bare, while others trim their pubic hair in fanciful heart shapes. One earth mother sports a luxuriant bush of curls I long to comb with my fingers. I know it's unprofessional to stare, but their nipples are my weakness, lined up before me like a buffet. I imagine sucking the dainty raspberry bonbons of one student, then tonguing the generous mocha-colored demitasse saucers of her neighbor.

Discreetly swallowing down the drool, I lead the class efficiently through the warm-up exercises: slow squeezes, butterfly wings and the elevator.

Squeeze and hold, ladies, squeeze and hold.

By the end our bodies are glistening with sweat; our eyes glowing with delicious exertion. Smiling, I announce a special reward for their hard work—a guest instructor who will help them get in touch with a new level of inner strength.

Adam steps from behind the folding screen in the corner, flourishing his magic brush. He takes his place before the first student, a small woman whose pale skin flushes when she's aroused. Now her chest is covered in telltale splotches of pink.

Gently, I instruct her to lie back and spread her legs for the new teacher.

Brow furrowed in concentration, Adam leans forward and inserts his brush delicately into her vagina. When he touches the tip to her inner labia, she moans.

"Let's breathe with her and be one with the sensation," I urge my other students, who stare with gaping mouths, transfixed by the intimate performance before them.

And so we all breathe together, our own pussies clenching in sympathy, as Adam traces the timeless circle of her flesh. Yet again, right before he reaches her clitoris, he stops.

Her eyes shoot open in dismay, but before she can protest, she climaxes, with a dainty, "Oh, oh, oh."

The next student in line immediately lies back without prompting. This lusty woman bellows when she comes. Some of the students are now rubbing themselves as they watch. In this manner, Adam works his way around the circle, stroking each woman to ecstasy with his artist's touch.

Of course, he saves me for last.

All eyes are upon me as I lie back and assume the position. Only when he kneels between my legs do I realize he is using a very special brush this time: a hot, thick tube of living flesh.

Even wielding this heavier instrument, Adam paints my circle with a knowing and sensitive touch. The room fills with soft moans—some my own—and I can hear the wet, clicking sounds of the women masturbating around me.

Will Adam complete the circle at last with his final touch of perfection? He draws achingly close to my clit, but again pulls away at the last moment, plunging deep into my orifice instead. This time I'm not passive. I clutch him with all of my power.

He makes a strange growl in his throat, part pleasure and part surrender.

A woman to my left makes a sound, too, one I recognize well: the sobbing cry of a female climax. As soon as her pleasure fades, the next student takes up the song. *I'm coming, oh, god...* Her neighbor joins in grunting like an animal. I know then we are all connected, the spasms of one woman's climax gliding smoothly into the pulsations of the next. When the orgasm finally reaches me, at the center of it all, the deep contractions resound inside me like a rich chord on a cathedral organ.

After my sessions, I'm so spent and deliciously sore, it's hard to believe it was all a fantasy.

Smiling, I reach over to my journal and draw another small circle, marking off another day until my lover and I really will be together.

When Adam finally called from the hotel in Kyoto, I nearly came from the sound of his voice alone. But I managed to play it cool through the inevitable "I missed you so much," and "I can't wait to see you."

"I missed you, too, but I kept myself surprisingly busy, especially in the evening," I said.

"Oh, how?" he asked, with just a hint of jealousy.

"I've been exploring the concept of *ensō*."

"Really? You've been practicing calligraphy?" He sounded pleased. "I'd love to see your work when I get home."

It was all I could do not to giggle. Only when we hung up did it occur to me he might be offended by my sensual interpretation of his spiritual practice. But Adam did have a sense of humor and he definitely appreciated sex. So I made sure to do extra practice sessions, just to make sure I was in tip-top shape for our reunion.

Forty-three hours later, a thinner, sexier, glowingly enlight-
ened Adam walked through security and grabbed me in a great
big circle of a bear hug. Fortunately, our apartment was only
twenty minutes from the airport, or we might have had to stop
at a motel on the way.

When we got home, Adam grabbed my hand and immediately headed for the bedroom. I shook free and strolled into the
living room instead.

"I want to show you my calligraphy first," I said, giving him
a mischievous sidelong glance. I gestured for him to take a seat
on the sofa.

"Oh, sure, great idea," he said, not quite hiding his disappointment. But as he started to sit down, I grabbed him by the
belt buckle.

"Take down your pants and underwear first," I said firmly.

He raised his eyebrows, but obeyed. He was already hard, of
course, and at the sight of his real "calligraphy pen," my pussy
contracted so sharply I flinched in surprise. Keeping my breath
steady, I knelt between his legs and took his cock in my mouth.

"Oh, god," he groaned, arching up.

If he was that easy to impress with a simple kiss, my next
trick was going to blow his mind. I decided it would be fitting to
start the art show with a preview of coming attractions. Accord-
ingly, I puckered my lips and began to squeeze his shaft with
the same rhythmic, gripping motions I used for my internal
exercises. Indeed, I was mirroring the same movements down
below—*clench, release, clench, release.*

I'd never heard Adam make such noises: surprise, pleasure
and distress all mixed together.

"Please, Maddy, stop," he begged. "You're going to make me
come. I don't want to come yet."

"Like it?"

"Yeah. I don't get the calligraphy connection, but that's okay," he breathed.

"Perhaps it lies beyond conscious awareness," I said, rising and leisurely unbuttoning my shirt. I stripped for him slowly, baring my breasts first and fingering my own nipples as I did each night when I masturbated. His gaze on my nude body was so smolderingly hot, I was afraid he'd raise blisters on my skin.

After a few teasing swivels of my hips, I straddled him on the sofa and immediately took him inside, purposely keeping my muscles loose and relaxed. This was a challenge, because his real cock was so hard and long and thick, I'd swear I could feel the length of him tickling my throat.

"Want to see my *ensō* now?"

Adam let out a hoarse little laugh. "Uh, no offense, but can it wait till later?"

"It doesn't have to wait. You see, I learned a lot about the magic circle while you were gone. How it represents so many things at once. Not just the void, but strength, elegance, the Universe, *enlightenment.*"

I gave him my best elevator squeeze, one, two, three, *hold.*

His eyes almost popped out of his head.

I squeezed again.

His head arched back and he let out a low, helpless, "Fuuuck."

I began to move, grinding my clit against his coarse hair on the downstroke, massaging his swollen shaft with my muscles as I rose.

Adam was beyond words now. His whimpers of protest let me know he was close to shooting his load. But I was close, too. The resistance of a thick, hard rod inside me definitely increased the effort—and the pleasure. I started in on the butterfly squeezes, a preview of climax in itself.

Adam grunted as if someone had punched the air out of him, and his hips bucked up into me. Before the vacation, it would have been way too soon for me, but now I closed my eyes and gave one last squeeze of his brush, the final stroke at last. My orgasm exploded deep in my belly, the spasms unbearably sweet and sharp, as Adam and I rode together to the finish.

"Like it?" I asked again as we rested afterward, our foreheads pressed together.

"A lot. I'd ask for details, but somehow I think another demonstration of your art might be more enlightening."

As he pulled me close for a kiss, I flashed on that moment at the Claremont spa when I started this journey, not quite sure where it would end. But now I knew.

When the circle is complete, you start again.

MOON TANTRA

Teresa Noelle Roberts

The full moon glints off the water and silvers the wet sand. Normally, the night beach would be quiet, but tonight it's crowded with people waiting to watch a total lunar eclipse.

It seems like a time for hushed expectancy, not a sound except the gentle surf. Instead, it's a party. Children shriek and dart at the water's edge. People are setting up late-night picnics. One group has laid out a deluxe spread—brie, sushi, champagne, fresh raspberries. "Some folks really know how to live," I whisper.

You squeeze my hand. "So do we." We have our own picnic in the small cooler you carry—lobster rolls and a bottle of sauvignon blanc—but I suspect you mean the wild time we had this afternoon in the whirlpool tub in our hotel room.

You set the cooler down, pull me close. After the hot-tub adventure, I thought I was sated, but I was wrong. A diffused lust spreads through me, suited to surreptitious caresses and the moonlight.

We shut out the night's human sounds, focusing on each other and on the music of the waves. Then a child darts too close, brushing me as he passes, and that moment is lost.

We walk perhaps a mile before we reach an area not yet colonized by families. We've been stopping frequently to kiss and touch, your hands taking advantage of the shimmering light to brush my nipples, mine using the shadows to stray to your crotch. I have a good idea why you want a spot that isn't in the center of the action. When you urge me to take off my panties, I bite my lip and clench in anticipation.

Still, as I wriggle them out from under my long skirt, I make a token protest. "Hey, I want to *see* the eclipse."

"Don't worry. You will. In style."

I know I'm not going to protest further. My panties, when I get them off, are damp.

We sit down on our blanket, leaning back against the cooler. You wriggle me into your lap, facing forward, and under the cover of my skirt, you pull down your shorts. A quick twist of my hips, a hand motion concealed by folds of gauze, and I sink onto your cock, reveling in the sudden stretched fullness.

Even when we're riding each other hard, this position draws things out. Trying to keep everything discreet will make it a protracted tease. The earth's shadow is starting its slow dance with the moon. Tonight we're taking it as slowly as they are.

I rock my pelvis slightly, making small circles around you. You sigh in my ear and grip me harder. At first, I want to move up and down on you until we both collapse in boneless pleasure. But then the slow rhythm of the rocking takes me to its own place.

Pleasure without peaking—it's oceanic, not like crashing waves but like the swells we can see in the distance when we take our eyes off the moon. I could go into a trance like this,

work the magic that enables us to walk the moon's path across
the water and reach another realm.

The water begins to darken from silver to pewter as the
shadow advances. Now about a quarter of the moon's bright
face is obscured. I turn to kiss you. Despite the awkward twisted
position, we fall into the kiss. "How long do you think we can
keep this up?" I say when we pause for breath.

"Let's find out." You're speaking through clenched teeth. "I
want to hold out until the moon's gone red."

I vaguely remember the moon doesn't redden until about an
hour after the first shadows are visible across its face. I've lost
track of how long we've been joined, but we've got a while to go.

The beach isn't as bright as it was. Under that cover, your
hands slip under my shirt to cup my breasts. You don't touch my
nipples, just stroke the warm valley beneath my breasts, enough
to tantalize me without pushing me too far.

Once, you run your fingers between them. Fire flares in my
pussy. I tighten, flutter my pelvis up and down. "You're thinking
of my cock moving between your breasts, aren't you?" you
whisper, lifting your hips to push into me. "Well, don't. Not
yet." You punctuate each of the last four words with thrusts that
leave me throbbing, close to orgasm but not there.

A smoky veil advances across the moon. Beneath that veil,
she is starting to blush.

On the verge of frenzy, I gesture toward that mere hint of
rosy glow. "Please," I beg. "Please."

"Not yet."

"I don't know how you're staying so calm," I manage to say.

"I'm not sure myself."

We fall silent again and almost still, watching the changing
face of the moon. The shadows move faster now. Soon, all but
one sliver in the upper quadrant is obscured. I mean to say

something poetic, but you move inside me at the same time. The thought flees as I start to shudder.

It's not exactly an orgasm, but it's ecstasy in its own right. First my belly muscles quiver, tiny, rapid contractions that spread throughout my torso. I feel my breasts shake against your hands. Then my legs begin to tremble in the same way.

The quivering in my belly moves deeper, from the muscles of my abdomen to my cunt. Release and yet not. The pleasure takes me to a higher plane of want even as it gives some relief to the building pressure.

"Wow," you breathe. "What was that?"

"I'm not sure," I say when I can talk again, "but I liked it." I relax against you, looking at the disappearing moon.

"It felt like you'd turned into a vibrator."

"It felt like that to me, too. Look—the moon's gone."

"She'll be back."

And sure enough, from beneath the cover of shadow, the moon slowly begins to reemerge. It is not so much that she is pushing the shadows away as she is glowing through them. "Soon," you say. "Fifteen, twenty minutes."

Can we stand it that long? I swivel around again, kiss you deeply. As we drink each other, your nails drive into my skin, as if that little bit of force helps you to keep control.

When we break apart, gasping, the moon is a quarter exposed and red as sin.

"Move," you say, the edge of tension in your voice a reminder to me that this must have been even more of an exercise in control for you than it was for me.

I begin to rise and fall on your cock.

I'm taken with an urge to lean forward so that I'm on my hands and knees, to drive back onto you. I'm about to do it when I remember that we're still in public. Granted, the people

around us are more interested in the moon than in their neighbors, but I have to maintain some level of decorum.

Thank goodness for full skirts and strong thighs. I squeeze
and release as I move, bigger circles now that let me push my clit
against your balls. You grip my hips and guide me. Underneath
the cover of my skirt, you are thrusting up into me.

I want to make crazy animal noises, claw at you, pound the
sand. I want to change our position so you're over me, driving
into my cunt with all your force, or I'm facing you, riding you to
glory. But that's too obvious. All I can do is grind against you.

It feels as if I've lived forever riding your cock, as if my whole
life has passed just on the verge of orgasm, in some place where
everything is molten red and there's nothing but your body
and mine, the moon and a soft shushing sound that may be the
waves or my own blood in my ears. And I think I wouldn't mind
spending the rest of my life this way.

The blood red moon shrugs off most of her veil of shadows.

As everyone's attention turns to the heavens, you drop your
hand between my legs, caressing my clit through my skirt.
"Now!"

Never mind what I was just thinking. I need to come.

The direct contact sears straight through me and I begin to
convulse. If I could, I'd howl. Instead, all the energy I'd normally
put into screaming goes into milking your cock with my contractions until you bite down on my shoulder to stifle your own cry.

As I return to myself, I feel my face is damp. I don't remember
weeping.

We shift positions so I am seated innocently between your
legs. Wrapping your arms and legs around me, you hold me even
closer than you did while you were inside me. We watch the sky
for another hour as the blushing moon and her dark lover finish
their long dance.

The beach is almost clear by the time the moon is back to normal. The sky to the east is already starting to bleach toward summer's early dawn. "Time to go back to the hotel?"

I yawn, snuggle against you. "Let's wait for sunrise. I've never seen sunrise over the ocean."

Your smile is tired but still lecherous. "I think by that time we can think of an appropriate way to greet it."

We curl up in each other's arms to nap until it's time for nature's next light show.

FEET ON THE DASHBOARD

Rachel Green

Jane checked the map again while she waited at the light, glancing down at the instructions she'd printed out in an enlarged font, the better to read while driving. It was a risk she was taking, meeting in person someone that she'd only met in a chatroom, but not one that she hadn't take a dozen times before.

The light changed to green and she pulled away again, looking on either side of the road for landmarks that were mentioned in the directions. Ah! There was one, a school. She nodded in satisfaction and looked to her left for a construction site. There! She pulled in below the sign advertising office space for rent and turned off the engine, letting out a deep sigh as she did so, stretching muscles that ached from a two-hour drive in the middle of the night.

With the radio playing softly in the background, she looked about her. The road beside her was silent, on one side the wall of the private school she'd just passed, the building site on her left. There were a few houses up ahead, mostly dark, but one or two windows still showed a light behind the drapes. Elizabeth must be behind one of those, she thought, though which, she had no idea.

It was not a bright move, traveling to meet someone she'd only ever typed messages to online without having any clue about the true identity of the woman behind the words. If it had been anyone else doing the same thing, she'd probably have given her a lecture about getting details and arranging safe calls, but she was terrible at taking her own advice and had done neither. The only verifiable information she possessed was the number of her assignation's mobile phone, and such numbers were as transient as the wind.

She was startled from her thoughts by a knock at the passenger window and reached across to open the door, her heart suddenly beating twice as fast. The woman who climbed inside matched the photograph Jane had received, and she relaxed and smiled, her self-assurance returning swiftly.

"Elizabeth, I presume?" The woman nodded.

"That is my real name, though not the one I'm normally known by. You, I'm rather hoping, are Jane?" She smiled as she spoke, and Jane was captivated by the deep magenta of her lips as she did so. *If the eyes are the windows of the soul, and the lips the windows of the body, then this woman most certainly has a body worth exploring in detail*, she thought.

She nodded and smiled. "Also my real name, though admittedly not the one currently showing on my driver's license," she said, starting the engine. "Do you have any suggestions for our destination?"

Elizabeth nodded ahead. "Go along here for about a mile and then turn right when you see a hotel with a turn lane."

They drove in an awkward silence for a few minutes, then

began with a little small talk, their joint nervousness showing through their outwardly calm exteriors

Elizabeth directed them along a small road through the grounds of a manor house, now publicly owned, and they pulled up in a gravel parking lot. There were several other cars there, each containing a couple behind steamed-up windows. Jane turned off the engine and grinned.

Elizabeth lunged, her mouth hungry for kisses, and Jane tasted the sweet aroma of whiskey on her breath as she twisted awkwardly in the seat to return the passion. There was fire in those kisses and Jane could feel her knickers getting wet as her desire increased, the flood of lubrication sudden and unexpected. She cupped her hand behind Elizabeth's neck and pulled her closer, their lips pressed tightly together and their tongues exploring each other's mouth. Jane's senses were swimming in hot desire as Elizabeth's perfume became heady in her nostrils. Lips became bruised as teeth scraped across them, and they paused for a moment to pull away and look at each other, then dove back as if one were a drug the other had become instantly addicted to. Elizabeth's hand fumbled in the waistband of Jane's jeans then shot upward to cup her breast. Jane gasped and flooded again, dipping her head to plant kisses on the bared flesh of Elizabeth's neck and shoulder, then pulling her dress down over one shoulder to expose her breast completely. Taking it into her mouth to suckle and tease to erection, she held it gently between her teeth as she flicked her tongue over the tip, causing Elizabeth to shudder with delight.

The car began to steam up, and they were enclosed within a womb of warmth, two women exploring each other for the first time. Jane's hand dropped to Elizabeth's legs and burrowed under the short black skirt, finding with delight that her new lover wore no knickers, and feeling the heat and dampness of a

cunt desperate to be fucked. She slid a finger inside and Elizabeth moaned. "Fuck me," she breathed. "Fuck me now."

Jane needed no further prompting and used her left hand
to pull back the skirt, dipping her head farther to taste all the
delights that Elizabeth had to offer. She ran her tongue over Elizabeth's labia, warm and full and tasting sweeter than honey on
her tongue. She sucked greedily and explored farther, hooking
her tongue underneath Elizabeth's hood and licking her engorged
clitoris, rolling her tongue into a tube and taking hold of the clit
as if it were a tiny penis and Jane's tongue a cunt.

Elizabeth groaned and spasmed, flooding Jane's fingers and
hand with her juices. Encouraged, Jane inserted a second finger
and then a third, massaging Elizabeth's G-spot from the inside
whilst her tongue deftly fucked her clitoris.

Elizabeth orgasmed again, her hand snaking down to unclasp
Jane's jeans and pull them partly down to find Jane just as wet
and ready as she was, her long, manicured nails digging into the
soft flesh just enough to make Jane grunt in a combination of
pain and excitement.

Elizabeth's fingers stroked Jane's cunt, eliciting groans, and
Jane contracted muscles that were aching to be used. She slipped
a finger inside and Jane gasped, unused to being on the receiving
end of sexual activity, and forced herself down onto Elizabeth's
strong fingers, moaning as she was massaged from the inside.
She used her free hand to yank down her jeans farther to allow
Elizabeth easier access. "Gods," she said, "that feels good."

Jane reciprocated by curling her right hand into a diamond
shape, with her thumb tucked tightly underneath her fingers, and
slowly pushed her whole hand inside Elizabeth, who clamped
her jaws together in pain but managed to gasp out "Don't stop!"
as she did so, raising one leg in the tight confines of the seat and
pressing it against the windshield. Jane pushed farther and was

rewarded by the feel of her whole hand being sucked in to the wrist. Once inside, Jane's hand curled naturally into the shape of a fist, pressed in on all sides by Elizabeth's cunt, and she pushed the other woman's cervix aside as she filled her more completely than a cock or strap-on could ever do.

She twisted her hand slightly, and Elizabeth almost screamed then came again, the juices squeezing out past Jane's wrist, and since they were under pressure, they sprayed the windshield and roof of the small car. Jane wasn't bothered and pushed Elizabeth into orgasm after mind-blowing orgasm until the muscles in her arm were screaming with exhaustion and she had to smile and ease her hand out again, not an easy task when Elizabeth's cunt had contracted sharply with each of nearly a dozen orgasms.

Jane sat back and stretched her arms out, grinning at the look of exhaustion on Elizabeth's face.

"I'm impressed," she said. "There're not many women who can both spray like that and have multiples without being in agony!"

Elizabeth laughed. "Who said I wasn't in agony?" she said, and leaned over for another kiss. "I'm so glad that you made the trip up here!" She pulled her dress back down and over her shoulder again and lay back in the seat, the flush of passion in her cheeks slowly fading.

Jane laughed before tidying herself up and cracking open the window slightly in an effort to dissipate some of the condensation on the windows. Out on the road, they could see the flashing lights of a police car as it turned into the parking lot, and she hurriedly fastened her seat belt and started the engine before they could be approached and questioned.

They drove back in companionable silence, constantly glancing at each other and grinning. All too soon, Jane pulled into the spot from which she'd collected Elizabeth.

"So," said Jane, as Elizabeth unbuckled her seat belt and reached across for a parting kiss, "shall we meet again?"

"Fuck, yes," Elizabeth replied, and then opened the door, climbing out and waiting until Jane drove off before she returned to her darkened house and sleeping family.

FROSTING FIRST

Lana Fox

Well, put it this way: what's sexier than dinner with guests; discussing wine, books, or the state of the nation; while the hottest man you've ever met kneels beneath the table biting the straps of your garter belt? Or, take it one step further. His tongue's right inside you, dipping in and out, circling sublimely, and there you are gripping the arms of your chair, pursing your lips to stop yourself from moaning; you begin to shudder, his hands are on your thighs, as your head falls back and your eyelids flutter. You can't keep from gasping as he finds the perfect rhythm, and you're close—so close!—to losing it completely.

"Are you all right?" asks your neighbor, fondling her pearls. "You're rather flushed. I'll get you some water."

"Please," you say.

She rises from her seat.

"You've turned quite a color," says her husband, from the other end of the long oak table.

"I'm sure."

You part your knees farther, arching as you come. "Sweet Jesus," you moan, your hands beneath the table, grabbing handfuls of your lover's hair.

Truth is, this all started with frosting—a birthday cake for your flatmate, Rose. She was in the living room chatting with her sister as you mixed the topping for a naked lemon bundt. Your man was with you—a new lover, then—and he kept dunking his fingers in the bowl, then licking at the frosting. You slapped his wrist. When you dipped your own index finger in and then ran it down his chin and sucked, like a porn star, at the sugary trail, he pressed a whole hand in the bowl of glaze, and, with the other, raised your shirt. See, you'd been taunting him all morning about your braless breasts, nipples hard beneath your clingy shirt, and as he pushed you back and peeled the whole thing off, you glanced toward the living room. The sound of Rose's voice through the open door—snippy, as usual—slyly turned you on.

"What if they come in?" you asked.

He raised an eyebrow. "Well?"

"Rose is kind of…uptight."

"Maybe we'll loosen her up."

You told him you were wet.

He flashed a sexy grin. "I'll make you wetter." You glanced back at your nipple, erect in the sunlight, and when he raised his hand from the bowl, palm and fingers gleaming, and plastered the glaze against your breast, you couldn't look away. Your breath ran quick at the cold, white layer, and the way your nipple, glossy now, was slick with sticky sugar.

"Lick it off," you whispered, as you arched against the worktop, offering your breast to his parted lips.

But though he glanced hungrily, he wouldn't give in. Not until the whole of you was frosted.

You can picture it now. You see yourself undressing, then climbing on the table, waiting on all fours with the sunlight on your back. The bowl's at your side, and the scent rises up in a sweet, powdered cloud. He walks around you, staring at your flesh, his cock growing hard, a mound in his jeans. "I'll smother you," he says, gaze burning. "Like a…like a meringue."

"You don't frost meringues."

He crosses the room and returns with a knife that's rounded at the tip and a wooden spatula he places in the bowl. "I'll frost what I like," he says. The knife sparkles in the sunlight. He leans on the table, raising your chin with the blade. "You're gonna be my project."

Your mouth waters.

"I'll fill you with cream."

"Yes, *chef*."

He scoops up some of the glaze on his knife then holds it up so you can lick along the blade. You do so, knowing how he loves it when you use your mouth. As the lemon icing tingles, tart on your tongue, he gives a jerky sigh, raises his jaw, and you let the frosting dribble from your lips so it slowly trails your throat. From there, it runs across your breast and he watches its path with a breathy moan. The way his lip seems to snarl at the corner says this won't be tame. "I'll make a cupcake of your pussy," he tells you.

In the next room, you can hear Rose disapproving of her sister's miniskirt, so you wink at your man and ask him how much cupcake he can handle.

But his finger's in the bowl and next thing you know, he's holding it toward you. "Swallow," he tells you.

You suckle his fingertip, lips rubbing round the joint, as your tongue flicks the sweet-sharp sugar from his nail. Then, with your free hand, you reach between his thighs, pressing his hard-on. He drops his head back, half shuts his eyes. "*So* dirty," he groans, pushing against you, as you massage his perfect length. You long to unzip him, take him in your mouth.

Then again, you also want him in control.

You let him go, moving back to position—doggy style, on all fours on the table—and though he lurches after you, still wanting your touch, his eyes soon return to your naked flesh. He begins to ice you, knife dipping in the mix and dragging oh-so-slowly down your spine. The wet steel makes you shudder; he pauses at your tailbone and dips the blade again. As he works your flesh, frosting you completely, he lingers at each sensitive spot. Where your sex meets your inner thigh, he pauses like an expert—with just another inch, he'd be frosting your pussy, and you are desperate for a touch of that dripping steel. So horny, in fact, that your mouth drops open and you swallow, your fore-arms shaking the table. When he slides the blade down the edge of your sex, you shift your clit toward it—just another inch, you think, before the blunt steel is sliding, wet, exactly where you need it, and the burn in you that's building so hard can be rubbed to a frenzy.

And yet, he pulls away.

"Be a good puppy," he whispers. He strips off his T-shirt. "Flip over now."

Yet again, you find you're drooling.

It isn't long before he's with you on the table, both hands covered in a fresh load of glaze, as you lie on your back waiting. You can smell the lemony frosting running down his wrists. He licks his thumb, eyes set on yours, then kneels up above you. Cupping your jaw with a dripping hand, he touches your breast with the other, and, with an index finger, circles your nipple. "Christ," he whispers. "Look how hard they are."

You tell him, "Touch them," but he idly circles.

"I love it when they're wet," he says, in a whisper.

And suddenly you're so desperate to have him touch you there that you grab his hand and splay it on your chest, arching and rubbing your breast against his palm. For a moment, it's exquisite. He gives a little snarl, and you notice him staring at his hand, while you can feel the wetness filling your sex and the tingles of pleasure where you rub your breast against him. Then suddenly he's ducking down, using his tongue, licking the frosting from your aching nipple and with the mess on his mouth and you, slick with saliva, you reach toward your clit. Oh, you ache to stroke it, if only for a second—your moisture's dripping down your thigh—but no, he grabs your arm. "Aren't we being dirty?"

"Of course we are," you say.

And that's when you know you'll be spanked.

When you were just a girl and your father grew fiercer, he argued nonstop with your mum about your diet. "She'll get fat, Val," he'd say. "You give her too much sugar."

"She doesn't eat badly," Mum would snap. "Besides, she's skinny. *Look*."

You'd sit on the couch between them as they bickered, ramming chocolate brownies into your mouth, or licking the buttercream from freshly frosted muffins, enjoying the feeling of it smearing down your chin. Sometimes, your father would notice you there.

"This," he'd say, "is exactly what I'm saying. You should see yourself, Jessie. It's disgusting." Rather than spanking you, he'd send you to your room, and in spite of the disappointment, you'd feel a strange heat—a sweet, slow creeping thing you'd yet to understand.

It isn't surprising that this flashes through your head while you lie on your back on the table, as your man rubs your sex with the slippery glaze and you hear someone moaning and realize that it's you. He parts your thighs, tells you you're gorgeous. The glaze slithers into you and then his tongue. Dipping right in, he finds the spot easily, flicking against you and spreading that glaze, which trickles, cool, mingling with your wetness, so you arch right back, slam your fists, cry his name.

You're in such heaven that your roll your head, and, in a flash, you see your flatmate's sister. She's leaning against the door frame: Pigtails. A flouncy skirt. Only twenty-one. Her fingers hover at her lip, a new darkness fills her gaze. That mouth, you note, is deliciously wide. Eyes glossing your body, she reaches under her skirt, and, as you roll and sigh, begins to touch herself.

Your man's fingers creep up your freshly creamed body, your skin tingling as his fingertips rub your slicked breasts. Suddenly, you know how you must look to your voyeur as she writhes against the door frame, head slamming back, pleated skirt lifted round her thighs, fingers working quickly underneath. This is why you tell your man, "Come on me. Now."

He glances up. His expression says you're filthy.

"I'm bad," you whisper.

Nearby, the girl groans.

Soon, you're bent right over—feet on the floor, hands on the table, your wetness and the frosting sliding down your flesh and behind you, your man with the icing-covered spatula waits, erect and ready, to teach you to be good. The scent is all animal, edged with sugar. At the doorway, the girl gives little gasps. You keep still, awaiting your man's swift punishment. The girl's eyelids flutter. She arches, hand busy.

"Now then," says your man, "we have an audience." Then he pulls back the spatula, gleaming with glaze, and thwacks it hard against your cheeks. The smacking sound is perfect. You give a little cry. He thwacks the tool again, over and over, so your body jolts hard, and the table shunts across the linoleum floor. Your torso's pulled with it, you're stretched from feet to ribs, yet he keeps on smacking you, and oh, the pleasure! The drying glaze, which clasps against your skin, when slapped with that wet spatula makes your flesh burn. "Come into me," you beg him. You're aching for his cock, but he keeps on spanking, the tool held tight.

When at last he drops the spatula, it skids across the floor toward the girl's feet. She watches you, with your hips thrown out, chin streaked with drool. Your man throws you across the sticky table and enters you quite suddenly, filling you entirely. Your jaw goes slack and you cry and laugh. With his hand splayed in the small of your back, and the drying frosting pinching your nipples, he thrusts, hips jolting against your ass. His cock ramming into you is slippery with frosting, and you still can't believe how perfectly you fit. He groans and grabs your thighs, fucking with such force that the table starts to shift across the room. You shift with it, and he lunges after, thrusting harder, grabbing your hair. He makes a rope of it, twisting your head back, and you see him there, beautiful, teeth biting at his lip, his glare ferocious, as he slams, again and again, building all that burn in you, that sweet-hot clench. As the girl's gasps rise higher, she parts her knees, rising up on the tips of her toes, a look of almost pain in her flickering eyes, and then you feel it, rising like flame, so you spread yourself wide for him, crying for him to do this, and it comes—in a thunder, rips through your body, and the world blurs around you, and you're high. He's thrusting so hard, moaning so loud, moving with such brilliance that he simply keeps you there, clinging to that feeling as the cries sound around you, and the whole damn room is gone.

You collapse.

He starts laughing, falls against your back; he whispers at your ear, "I think we're in trouble."

For there, behind the blushing girl, is Rose, your flatmate, her hands on her hips, a sneer on her mouth. She glares from her sister, who snorts and giggles, to your man and then to you, sucking at her teeth. "I—I don't know what to say," she blurts. "Really, it's...revolting."

You give an empty shrug.

Your man follows with a wave and says, "Hey, happy birthday, Rose," and you slap his wrist. You'll recall it took you months to win Rose back, to persuade her you hadn't meant to invade—but you never did get her to join in.

What a shame. She might have liked it.

So anyway, back to when he's underneath that long, oak table, while your guests flap about you offering you water, and Christ, good Christ, you let those other waters flow...and in that instant you cry his name.

It's a shock. He bumps his head.

The wife crouches down, raises the tablecloth.

"Why, hello there, neighbor," you hear him say.

You laugh out loud at his timing, his wit.

Later, in bed, you'll ask your man if these activities are wrong. "You know what they say about 'delayed gratification'? Maybe we should wait for sex. Allow it to *build*?"

To this, your man will push back your hair, a saucy look of pleasure on his face. "We're bad," he says. "Accept it. We like our frosting first."

ALL SHE WANTED

Andrea Dale

When you're pregnant, you worry about all sorts of things: Will the baby be born with extra toes? Will I crave pickles and chocolate ice cream—at the same time? What if we give it the wrong name and it hates us forever? Where the hell did *those* breasts come from?

The answers to those types of questions can be found in your average book for expectant parents, books that speak in soothing language to assuage your fears.

Such books don't address certain other crucial questions, such as: By what month should one avoid rope bondage? Do nipple clamps adversely affect milk production? How will my raging hormones affect my ability to enter sub-space?

I joke about it, make light of it, as I do with anything that scares me. Avoidance, my husband Dan says when he catches me doing it. I should face my fears, according to him. Then he devises some sort of devious torture—sometimes just a spanking, sometimes much, much more—to teach me not to do it.

Of course, that never works. For one thing, everybody has his own way of dealing with fear. For another, I *like* being tied up and whipped and teased and tortured. If I didn't, we wouldn't be in this relationship, where in the bedroom he calls all the shots.

When we found out I was pregnant, however, everything changed.

Don't get me wrong—my first priority is the baby. I'm not going to do anything stupid. But sex doesn't stop when you're pregnant, and kinky sex doesn't have to stop, either.

There's no telling Dan that, though. I appreciate the depth of his caring, but I'm going a little crazy here.

The hormones rage through me like a tropical storm, and Dan understands that, so even when I make the jokes in the hopes of baiting him, he doesn't follow through, not the way we're used to.

I want to be caned until I'm dizzy with pain and desire, not gently spanked after I've been carefully arranged on special pillows. I want to be forced to wear that awful ball gag that makes me drool, that tastes faintly like rubber no matter how many times we wash it. I want some serious bondage and teasing and to be made to come over and over until I'm limp and sore and barely breathing.

And while we're at it, I want an Oompa Loompa and I want it now!

See? There I go. If Dan hears me and tells me to watch it, and I mouth off with *Whatcha gonna do, spank me?*, then what *is* he going to do?

Not. Very. Much.

I suppose I shouldn't complain. Even without the hard-core bondage and exquisite pain play, we haven't gone completely vanilla. Dan's a master at the head fuck, too, and sometimes threats and suggestions and tales spun about impossibly filthy scenes can be amazingly effective, especially when combined with blindfolds and delayed orgasms. (Not too delayed, though, just in case it causes my blood pressure to spike oh-point-two degrees.)

It was during one of those sessions that Dan ordered me to bring home a play partner for us.

Multiple partners weren't new to us. We had a small but fun network of friends who on random occasions overlapped; we'd done your usual share of romping in public dungeons. I enjoy the taste of a woman, the feel of her mouth on me, the sounds she makes when she comes—and the sounds I make when she makes me come.

In my haze of arousal, I agreed. (Of course I agreed. I never argued with Dan, unless I was serious enough to haul out my safeword.)

Fact is, most of us will agree to things in the haze of arousal, more so if you're a sub and you're flying. It was only after the fact, when I'd come back to earth and had a warm shower and a nap, that reality hit.

At four months, it wasn't like I was waddling yet, but I felt fat...bloated...missing a defined waistline. Pale blue spider veins crept and twined up my legs, and my complexion was a teenager's nightmare.

Oh, sure, the nausea had finally passed (hallelujah!) but it had been replaced with the twin gastrointestinal joys of heartburn and gas.

And my nipples, my wonderful sensitive nipples that loved being twisted and tweaked and clamped within an inch of their lives? At first their being constantly tender was a turn-on. Now...well, I hadn't known there was a point beyond pleasurable nipple pain. (Not all pain is arousing. Slamming my fingers in the car door does not make me come.) Dammit.

Add the hormones into all that, and self-conscious didn't

even begin to describe it. Hel-*lo*, quivering mass of insecurities.

I didn't want anybody else to see me like this. (Not naked in a scene, anyway. Seeing me dressed at the grocery store was okay. On good days. Maybe.) But I'd agreed to do it, and besides, it was just about the stupid hormones, right?

I ended up taking Lauren out for coffee and broaching the offer to her. She'd recently split up with her husband, and I thought she could use some cheering up. Yes, I really thought that. That mothering instinct must have already been kicking in.

Lauren, cute and curvaceous, with perfect skin and flowing black hair, was delighted and enthusiastic.

I felt both relieved (I'd accomplished what Dan asked me to do) and nervous in a way I hadn't felt since…well, as long as I could remember. We'd played with Lauren and her husband years ago but never just with her. That shouldn't have made a difference.

The hormones suggested otherwise.

It was stupid, I knew, to feel jealous that I was drinking sparkling cider while Dan and Lauren sipped wine (one glass only— alcohol and kink do *not* mix well) as we discussed the things we needed to negotiate, like boundaries and safewords. I felt like a kid at the adult's table.

Just to illustrate how conflicted I was, I also felt incredibly horny. I *wanted* to play, and I harbored the hope that somehow, this would make Dan loosen up a little and give me what I really wanted. Plus, it had been a while since I'd been with another woman, and there was all that excitement building….

We haven't yet turned the playroom into the baby's room, because the crib will be in our room for the first few months, at least. There was something oddly calming, almost soothing, about walking in there. I had the sense that for the next few hours, I didn't have to worry about a damn thing; Dan would be in charge, call the shots, make the decisions.

I trusted him completely in that regard. It was why our relationship worked.

Dan settled himself into a chair and ordered us to strip each other, slowly. I fought back feelings of self-consciousness, and Lauren's murmured approval of my newfound impressive cleavage helped. Dan warned her about how overly sensitive my breasts were even as he encouraged us to play with each other. We both understood that it was a show for his benefit; coming without permission was not an option.

With hands and mouth, she whispered and tickled across my nipples, a flick of a tongue here, a brush of a thumb there, a butterfly kiss. My belly contracted as I tangled my hands in her silky hair and watched, fighting the need to let my eyes flutter shut.

My pussy lips slickened. Already I could smell our joint arousal, the sweet spicy scent of mingled desire. I wanted to taste her, but only if Dan okayed it.

Just hands for now, though; I dipped my fingers into her and brought them to my lips. Lauren leaned toward me and together we kissed and licked her juices away.

Teasing, caressing and then grinding our crotches together, mine neatly trimmed, hers waxed smooth.

Now Dan wanted attention, and at his command we gave it to him, undressing him and kissing and licking him. He particularly liked it when we kissed each other around his burgeoning cock, and I particularly liked it when he threaded his fingers through my hair and tugged the strands to guide me.

When Dan ordered us to stop, he picked up my favorite flogger, the expensive kangaroo leather one with knots in the tails. My pussy clenched and my heart soared, or maybe it was the other way around. Finally!

But he didn't tell me to bend over. Instead, he commanded Lauren to present her pretty little ass.

Okay, fair enough: guests first. He'd be a bad host otherwise.

When he handed me the flogger, I stared at it like I'd never seen it before, like it was an alien object. I almost giggled, part of my mind imagining the stupid, blank look on my face. What, exactly, was I supposed to do with *this*?

Dan broke through my confusion. "Go on, honey," he said. "Have fun. Warm her up for me."

We'd tried switching before, so I suppose it wasn't an entirely foreign concept, but quite frankly, it wasn't my thing. Because Dan was ordering me to do it, though, I did.

I kept it pretty light, not familiar enough with this side of things to know how to gauge the intensity of my strokes. Lauren still enjoyed it, though. She mewled with pleasure, wiggling her ass as it blushed beneath the strands. Her legs were parted (Dan had nudged them apart with the whip handle before giving it to me) and her cunt shone. I knew she wanted to bring her thighs together, squeeze out some pleasure. I didn't blame her.

I wanted that, too. I wanted to be flogged and to be naughty and grind against something and have Dan stop and make me beg for my punishment.

I was jealous in a way I'd never been jealous in a scene before. Oh, I've been *envious*, in a "I want what she's having" kind of way, but then there was always the possibility that I *was* going to get what she was having, or even better.

Even as Dan took the whip from me, I knew he wasn't going to use it on me. As he struck Lauren and she howled with delighted pain, I just felt sad that Dan needed another woman to top because he didn't want to top me. I couldn't give him what he needed.

So when he paused to stroke between Lauren's legs and said, "Oh, good girl," in that tone that he's always used with me, the twisting pain in my stomach wasn't just from the churning acidic bath in there.

I broke down and cried, and in between my sobs I blurted out my safeword.

Once we were out of the playroom, away from the scene, I calmed down. Stupid hormones. That's the excuse I used, anyway. Lauren was sweet and understanding, and as much as I wanted to hate her for it, I couldn't. She kissed me before she left, told me I was gorgeous and sexy and that she wanted to play again sometime.

I wasn't so far gone that I couldn't feel an appreciative tingle of desire for that.

Dan, too, was understanding, not that I'd expect him to be anything different. "I thought if you couldn't bottom as heavily, you'd enjoy a little topping," he said.

Yeah. He'd set this whole thing up *for* me. Take that, Miss Bundle of Insecurities.

We talked it out, and he admitted maybe he'd been too gentle with me, although he also admitted he really was concerned about overdoing it.

He drew me a bath with lavender and eucalyptus bubbles and told me to relax while he came up with a new plan. Something I'd definitely enjoy, he said in that deliciously threatening dom voice.

He also told me I could fantasize and masturbate if I wanted to but not to let myself come.

Oh, he knows me too well.

I couldn't imagine the depths of his deviousness, and that always aroused me even more.

Then I was out of the tub and into the bedroom, where he buckled my wrists to the poles at the foot of the bed.

He flogged me, oh, hallelujah, yes. Not as hard as I wanted, maybe, but combined with his words—my Master of the Head-Fuck indeed—he had my juices flowing.

"You did a good job on Lauren, but you were too gentle with her. Someday I'm going to ask her to use the flogger on you, and you'd better believe she's going to pay you back for being too nice."

He went on to tell me how he'd show her how to whip me first, so I'd get a double helping, and probably a paddle afterward on my extrasore striped and dotted flesh.

It let me imagine how that would feel and heightened the sensations now.

Then, the pièce de résistance: when he brought it out, I recoiled. Damn him.

Anal play was the only thing he'd ever had to talk me into. I don't know why, but I hated it with a passion that made it all the more exquisitely exciting when we did it. An anal orgasm sent me through the roof like no other, because I was helpless to stop him from fucking my ass with that bright blue devil of a plug.

"Thank god the hemorrhoids haven't started yet." Oops! That popped out of my mouth before I could catch it.

He brought out the ball gag I'd missed so much, and I melted a little inside.

Then his breath was hot on my neck while he told me not only what a good girl I was, but a naughty girl, a filthy girl, and he was sliding the lubed plug in, and I forgot about being bloated and tired and insecure.

If I'd been able to speak, I probably would've said something like, *Mama's comin' home!*

Instead, I just flew.

MAKING SHAPES

Lily Harlem

'm coming."

"No, hold off."

"I can't."

"Just a few more seconds."

"Shit, it's too much."

"Try, otherwise we'll have to start over." I looked up at Theo Driver's face hanging over the side of my custom-made bench. His thick black brows had knotted over scrunched eyes, and his teeth tugged at his bottom lip. "It's nearly done," I encouraged. "It's quick setting, this stuff, just think about your Gran knitting or something."

A muscle flexed in his cheek and his fingers paled as he gripped the white padding just inches from my upturned face.

I braced under the weight of the seaweed-based molding paste I'd positioned against his erect cock, which was poking through a hole in the bench. The bucket had to be kept dead still to get a perfect cast of his penis, and much as it would be a perk of my unusual job to witness his pleasure, I knew from experience a shot of come in the mold would distort the end result, and we'd be back at square one, redoing his cast.

I studied the clock above the closed door to the shop front. "Time," I said fifteen seconds later. "Pull slowly up from the bench in a straight line."

"Thank fuck for that." He lifted his hips upward, opened his eyes and fixed his brooding, somewhat glazed focus on mine. "Oh, shit." He suddenly winced and scrabbled to face shelves containing body molds in various stages of completion. His broad shoulders hunched and he grabbed his dick as a violent shudder snaked up his spine.

I clutched the bucket to my chest and straightened from my squatting position under the bench. My ears pricked with delight as his deep grunt filled the studio. He tried to internalize a moan but he was a big, testosterone-fueled man, and there was nothing he could do to stop even harnessed pleasure from rattling like an echo in a cave.

"Why did you look at me like that?" he muttered, grabbing a wad of tissues I kept next to the bench.

"Like what?" My own heart rate was racing so loud I was sure he'd be able to hear it.

"All pretty and girly." He didn't look at me as he wiped himself. "Shit, that never happens." He stood and tucked his still impressively big penis into his boxers and pulled up his jeans. "I'm usually in perfect control."

"Of course," I said, struggling to maintain professionalism as he stepped around the bench and towered over me. "But it's good you were so near the edge of orgasm when we took the casting." I nodded down at the white chalky substance revealing the perfect indent of his erect cock. "It means we've immortalized you at your most...spectacular."

His irritated expression cracked into an amused grin. "Yeah, Emma will like it."

"She's a lucky girl." As soon as the words fell from my mouth I realized it had been the wrong thing to say. "I...I mean...what I wanted to say is...you're a very thoughtful man, to think of her needs at a time like this." I tried to shift my gaze from his intense scrutiny, but his coal black eyes had captured mine and refused to let go.

"Yeah, well, I need her to have something to play with while she's backpacking." He stepped closer and his musky male scent encircled me, a hot cloud of recently released desire lying in the air like salt blowing on an ocean breeze. "I don't want her running off with a surfer dude, do I?"

"I'm sure she wouldn't."

He reached out and caught a wild, red ringlet that had escaped my ponytail. "I'm just wondering what I'm going to play with whilst she's gone." He tucked the wayward curl behind my ear. "I've never cheated but..."

I swallowed, my mouth suddenly dry. "But you're a man," I said, stating the fact my hormones were screaming about, "with needs; perhaps Emma could come to Making Shapes and get a body mold done for you. I do a great range of very intimate, very user-friendly products."

He stepped away with a derisive snort. "Not my thing. I prefer hot flesh writhing under me." He reached for his wallet, his expression all business. "How much do I owe you?"

"Nothing for now." I walked over to a long, steel counter and put down the bucket with its precious contents. "You can settle up when you collect the finished product."

"When will that be?"

"In about a week, is that all right?"

"Yep, she goes in ten days so a week should be fine."

He pulled open the door and strode from the studio. My eyes were irresistibly drawn to his perfect, denim-encased rear. I smoothed my dusty hands together, imagining what his skin would be like to touch: warm and soft but at the same time bubbling with powerful muscles lurking just below the surface. I'd meant what I said about Emma being a lucky girl. Theo Driver was one hell of a man and if he were mine, there was no way I'd be hopping off to Australia for six months. No way on earth.

Two weeks later I held Theo Driver's cock in my hand as November rain whipped the skylights above my studio. Theo hadn't been back to collect his body molding, so I guessed Emma had come to her senses about leaving such a prime specimen all alone.

I thought unenthusiastically about the lonely evening ahead in my small King's Road flat. I really should start charging customers when they came for their sittings. That way I might make enough money to buy somewhere bigger, or even take a holiday and get some sun.

I sighed and passed the cock from one hand to the other. I was pleased with the finished product. I'd spent a considerable amount of time perfecting the deep rose-petal shade; shadowing the bulging, twisting veins along the shaft and adding his two small freckles onto the wide smooth head, just to the right of his slit. He was circumcised and I liked that; the cock looked neat and clean, and with the new glaze it felt smooth as glass when I ran my fingers up and down the length of it.

I curled my thumb and index finger around the base, just above where the first inch of his ball sac was molded. My fingers wouldn't meet; his trunk was so wide, so thick. My breath quickened as I imagined him penetrating me; how would he fit? I was little, five foot two, and he must be well over six feet and with all that raw power surging behind a hungry penis, he'd surely split me in half. A buzz sparked in my clit. Like a tuning fork tapping against me, its resonance hummed through my neglected but sensitive flesh. Theo was on a whole different size scale to me; it was a wonder we were the same species living on the same planet.

A sharp gust of wind rattled the skylight. I looked up into the London night sky and saw the moon peek through a racing cloud before being engulfed in blackness once more. Maybe I should take Theo's dick home tonight, give it a trial run, test its dildo qualities and test my abilities to take it into my body. Emma would never know, Theo would never know; even if he collected it tomorrow, it would wipe clean good as new—a quick rinse and a polish and no one would be any wiser.

I bounced its substantial weight in my palms and a new thought popped into my head. Would it fit in my mouth? I didn't know if my jaw could stretch that wide, if my teeth would part sufficiently to house such a beast.

I glanced at the door leading to the shop front. It was a little ajar, but anyone shouldering the weather and passing my display windows wouldn't see into the studio, and I'd locked the front door earlier when I'd shut the shop. I swept my tongue over my lips, curiosity eating me up the way I wanted to eat him up. I would give it a quick try here, just to see.

I lifted the dick to my face, slit upward. It shone like marble in the stark overhead lights and reflected the steel shelves to my left. I closed my eyes and let the cool head press against my top lip, poked out my tongue and rimmed the groove of skin under the base of his glans. I tried to remember Theo's heady mix of pheromones swirling around me to imagine his flavor: musky and manly, erotic and hot.

I couldn't wait any longer. I stretched my jaw wide and slid the head onto my tongue. My jaw gave a soft click as he smoothed in. My knees turned weak and I pictured his face contorted with the effort of not coming: eyes squeezed shut, teeth dragging at his lip and his breaths sharp and shallow. I sent a hand to my breast as I slid him to the back of my throat and tweaked my nipple to a painful point through my sweater. He hit delicate flesh and as I struggled with my gag response, I imagined his hands on me, fondling my breasts, cupping the nape of my neck, stroking the corners of my poor stretched lips.

I moaned, slid him out and then back in again, the dildo warming and becoming coated in my saliva, its eternal hardness a celebration of my craft. I sent a hand to the waistband of my jeans, popped the metal button and shoved my fingers down my knickers. I kept my eyes shut tight, only the sound of the wind and the rain intruding upon my fantasy of having Theo thrusting into my mouth.

My clit was on fire, swollen and demanding attention as my fingertips began deep, urgent rotations. I didn't know if I could stay standing even though I was leaning against the counter. My legs were like jelly, my spine desperate to curl forward for the pressure and rhythm of my own ministrations. I opened my eyes to the harsh light of the room and spotted the molding bench. I needed to lie down but that would put me in view of the shop front. I should just shove the cock in my bag and head home where I could play to my heart's content. But the cock had come to life slipping in and out my mouth, teasing me with how delicious it would feel shunting in and out of my pussy.

Fantasy was what I needed…now.

I took a few wobbly steps to the door, banged a flat palm against it to shut it nearly flush then staggered to the bench, pulling at my jeans zipper as I went. I needed them off, or at least round my ankles to have any chance of accommodating this monster.

My pussy pumped with blood and my head felt dizzy with the thought of what I was about to do. I gave the cock one last slide down my throat, really deep this time so I could hardly drag air in. My fingers found the entrance of my pussy and I shoved up, surprised by how wet and swollen I was. I surged in, over and over, stretching in preparation. Theo's cock was all I could think of.

BANG. BANG.

The glass front door of the shop rattled under the force of a fist.

BANG. BANG.

My eyes flew open and I stared at the not-quite-shut wooden door between me and the shop front. Oh, my god! A mental picture of what I must look like invaded my brain: trousers round my ankles, one hand shoved up my pussy and a dildo pounding the back of my throat.

I pulled Theo's dick from my mouth and dropped it on the bench. With wet fingers I yanked up my jeans, struggled with the zipper and wiped my lips on my sleeve. I took a shaky step forward. "Open up, I know you're in there." A deep voice penetrated the shop.

I stopped in my tracks.

"The studio lights are on, open up." *BANG. BANG.*

A wave of nausea swept through my stomach as a wash of anticipation flooded my pelvis. I smoothed back my hair, set my face to business mode and pushed into the darkened shop front.

Theo Driver was standing at the door, broad palms pressed against the wet glass and his shadowed figure backlit by an amber streetlamp as wind lifted leaves and litter around his feet.

He wore a long trench coat and rain dripped from his hair, hung in his brows and ran from his chin.

"Making Shapes is closed," I said, walking toward the door.

"Open up." He glared at me through twinkling drips, his jaw set obstinately. "Now."

"Why?" I put my hands on my hips determined to project an equal degree of stubbornness. For all he knew, I could have been in the middle of a very intimate molding or a very intricate piece of artwork.

"Emma has gone."

"But you didn't collect your cock…I mean your…your body sculpture."

"There was no point, we finished, or rather *I* finished it with her."

"You did. Why?"

"Can we have this conversation inside?" His scowl deepened and his eyes bored into mine. "In case you hadn't noticed, the weather's not so good out here." As he spoke, he was lit with a brilliant flash of lightning followed by a violent clap of thunder that shook my display sculptures on their stands.

Startled, I jumped forward. My hands scrabbled with the lock and I tugged the door open. Theo stepped in along with several tumbling leaves that settled around his feet.

"Thanks," he said as I relocked the door.

I shrugged. "What can I help you with, Mr. Driver?"

A cocky smile tickled one side of his mouth and with a rush of panic I wondered if he'd seen me with his glazed cock in my mouth and my fingers jamming into myself, preparing for a trial entry of his body art. But no, how could he have seen? There were only skylights in the studio, and the door had been more or less shut. I beat down a blush. He couldn't possibly know what I'd been doing when he arrived.

"Well, to start with, I'd like my body molding, if it's ready."

"Yes, of course." I indicated for him to go into the studio.

He turned and walked ahead of me. The eye magnetism to his butt returned and even though he was wearing a long coat I couldn't help feasting on the thought of those hidden orbs of delectable flesh.

As we stepped into the brightly lit room my lust-frazzled brain suddenly remembered where I'd left the molding—abandoned on the central bench, flattening a thick crease my shuffling naked buttocks had created.

"Is that it?" His eyes widened. "Is that mine?"

"Er, yes." Its deep pink color looked startling against the crisp white sheets and it shone brightly, sparkling as if dripping with moisture—my moisture.

"Why is it there?" He turned to me.

"I, er, just finished it, it's drying under the lights." Improvising, I pointed to the fluorescent strip-light dangling directly above the bench. "It's a good job you're late picking it up. I've been so busy it wouldn't have been ready for Emma."

Theo snorted at the mention of her name.

"So what happened between you guys?" I was keen to change the subject.

He dragged his arms from his wet coat and draped it over a stool. "I offered to go with her to Australia." He reached for a towel lying by the sink and gave his short turf of jet black hair a vigorous rub. "I've got my own web design business. It would've only taken a couple of hours a day online to keep clients happy and sites ticking over."

I tipped my head for him to continue.

"She said no." He tossed the towel aside. "She wanted to travel alone." He shrugged his wide shoulders, which were encased in a thick gray jumper. The roundness of his deltoids bulged at his shoulders and several dark hairs peeked from the neck. "I realized Emma always wanted to do things alone. I rarely slotted into her daily routines or plans. So what was the point? Our relationship was going nowhere so there seemed nothing to gain from waiting six months..." He stepped closer. "Especially when someone else had caught my attention."

A shiver ran up my spine as I recalled his earlier comments about wanting something to play with. Did he want more than that now he was single? Was he really interested in me? We'd only met twice before, once to organize the appointment and then for me to cast his dick in a mold and watch him come. It was a fairly unusual couple of meetings, but just the same I'd been unable to stop thinking about him; did he feel the same way about me?

I felt myself sway toward him. Heat radiated from his damp body onto mine; he was practically steaming in the heat of the studio. He licked his lips and bent his head, looked at my mouth like a starving man. Was he going to kiss me?

He stepped away, to the bench.

I dragged in much-needed oxygen; I'd been holding my breath.

He picked up his cock and passed it between his hands. His eyes narrowed and his mouth set in a straight line.

"Do you like it?" I asked, hoping the squeak in my voice wouldn't betray just how much I liked it, or just what I'd intended doing with it only minutes before.

His brows lifted but he offered no comment.

"It's top quality glaze, should last for years, it's practically shatterproof unless you run a car over it or maybe a tractor or a motorbike or..."

"It's wet." His gaze snagged mine. "It's wet and...and warm, too."

"I told you, it's drying, it's not quite ready." I thrust my hands on my hips and projected my aloof, misunderstood artist persona.

His dark eyes roamed my body and my aloofness disintegrated like a summer puddle. He drank me up as though he could see right through my clothes and suddenly I was aching with longing. He chewed on his cheek as his eyes settled on my chest, and I knew without looking my nipples were standing to attention, plainly visible through my sweater.

"It's fit for purpose then?"

"Pardon?"

"The molding, my cock, it's tough, it can take a bit of rough treatment."

"Yes, money back guarantee." I smiled. "If it breaks I'll redo you."

He nodded sagely and lifted the penis to his face, much the same way I had. But Theo didn't put it in his mouth. Instead he held the shaft under his nose and sniffed it like an expensive cigar. "Still smells new," he said in a low voice.

"It is new, brand new."

"Is it?" His sudden sharp gaze dared me to lie. "Are you sure it hasn't been used for anything?"

"Of course it hasn't." I frowned "What, doesn't it look like yours or something?"

"That's not what I meant." He pointed the cock at me. "I know it's mine, it's even got my freckles on the head—you've a very fine eye for detail."

"Thank you." I folded my arms over my breasts. "Now, Mr. Driver, I'll box it and you can settle your account at the till." I moved to the shelving unit where I kept packaging.

Suddenly he was behind me, his chest pressing into my back and his hot breath seeping down my neck. "I want to know where it's been…what you've done with it," his deep voice whispered into my hair. "I feel…violated knowing you've had a part of me to play with, treat as your own, and I don't know what went on."

I tried to twist and face him but he captured me in thick arms and held me facing my store of boxes.

"Where has it been?" he murmured, pulling me tight against the length of his body. I dragged in a shocked breath. He was fully erect, hard as steel and prodding my lower back. "You smell of sex and you're here alone."

"No, I don't."

"You can't deny it," he murmured. "It's pouring off you like perfume. Woman and spice, lust and need, it's around you like an aura, and since my cock was on the bench, I'm guessing you two were entertaining one another."

My stomach flipped. I'd been rumbled. He was right, there was no denying it.

"My cock doesn't smell of pussy so I'm guessing it wasn't here." He pressed the tip of the fake dick against my mound, sending just the right amount of pressure through my jeans to my already excited clit. I let out a whimper and rested my head into the crook of his shoulder.

"Perhaps it was here." He ran it up over my sweater and nestled it between my tits.

"No," I said watching the freckles wink at me.

"Maybe here." He spun me round, captured my face in his hand and with a squeeze on either side of my mouth forced my jaw open.

I went to mutter a protest but as soon as the sound emerged he poked the head of his dick into my mouth. My eyelids fluttered shut as I remembered the shape and size of it and the yearning it had generated in my pussy.

"Perfect fit," he said, pulling out.

I opened my eyes, held his unwavering eye contact and poked out the tip of my tongue. Very slowly I licked his slit as though savoring ice cream.

His eyes clouded and like a tornado blasting my body, his dark, heady and downright predatory lust hit me full on.

In that moment, I knew we were going to fuck.

I tipped forward and swallowed the cock again, even deeper this time and watched with satisfaction as his mouth slackened and he let out a moan of approval. "Bloody hell, you're good," he said, grinding his real cock against me and hitting my stomach because of his height. "I knew the moment I came so hard just by looking into your eyes you were special."

He pulled the fake cock out and his lips hit down on mine, hard and insistent. His tongue forced past my teeth but I fought him at his own game, plunged my tongue into his hot, black-coffee wetness and wrapped my arms around his neck.

Big, solid biceps squeezed my torso and my feet lifted from the floor. "You want the real thing?" he said between kisses.

"Yes," I managed. "But not in my mouth."

"Where?"

"You know where."

He sat my behind at the feet end of the high bench and cupped my face. "I want to hear you say it."

My hands drifted down his rock solid pecs to his belt with filthy intentions oozing from my fingertips.

"No." He grabbed my wrists. "Not until you tell me where you want me."

"I want you..." I licked my lips and narrowed my eyes. "In my pussy."

"Cunt," he said in a voice so deep it was a growl. "I want you to say 'cunt.'"

"Okay...cunt...I want your cock in my cunt." My heart surged with the dirtiness of the words. Saying them in front of Theo, about Theo, was like having a shot of adrenaline injected into my clit.

In a sudden frenzy, he dragged my jeans and knickers from my hips and whisked them so hard from my ankles he yanked me to the tip of the bench. He kissed me again, hard and appreciatively, sucking and licking my neck, nipping my nipples through my sweater. I ran my hands over his shoulders and lay back. His bites stung but I knew what was coming would hurt a whole lot more.

His hands were fiddling under the bench. I heard the clunk of unfolding metal and the next thing I knew my feet were simultaneously lifted into the stirrups I kept for making vulva moldings, perfectly positioned to keep ladies' legs high and dry with their butts perched over the edge.

Theo stepped between my spread legs and stared down at my intimate folds. If I hadn't been so insanely turned on, I would have squirmed with self-consciousness at being so exposed. "I've been vulnerable in front of you," he said quietly. "And at your mercy. It was the hottest thing I've experienced in a long time, and I want you to experience that, too." He reached out a finger and brushed it through my tight curls of scarlet pubic hair. "Glad it's your natural color," he said with an approving nod.

My hips twitched as he sank to his knees and flicked his tongue over my desperate clit. I groaned and stretched my arms above my head as a roll of thunder rattled the studio.

His rain-cool fingers rimmed my entrance, exploring and spreading my juices into every secret place. He began to suck greedily on my nub, and I whimpered and shoved my hips onto his face as far as constraints would allow.

"Don't come, not yet," he ordered, licking his way down my

inner thigh. "Not until I say, just like you controlled me."

"But…"

His tongue tangled with my clit and he began stretching my vagina, pumping in two thick fingers and scissoring them to release tight tissue. My flesh quivered. The sensations were overwhelming; an orgasm was beginning to build, preparing to erupt.

His hot body loomed over mine again, and I groaned at the loss of his expert attentions between my legs. He kissed my mouth and as I tasted myself on his lips, I felt the cool head of the dildo at my entrance before it drove in an inch.

"No…I want the real thing," I said, squirming.

The dildo slipped down and exerted a firm pressure on my anus. In reflex I bucked at the shocking sensation but was unable to move away.

"What about here?" he rumbled.

"No," I whimpered, my mind spinning at the dirty, forbidden yet disturbingly exciting suggestion.

"Next time," he said, his voice low and decidedly dangerous. "You'll take us both."

My sphincter fizzed at the impossible thought of being fucked and buggered at the same time.

Hail pounded the skylights.

"Please," I begged, my voice needy and desperate even to my own ears. "The real thing…in my cunt."

The dildo clattered to the floor. With an unintelligible grunt he unzipped his trousers and shoved the hot, hard head of his glorious prick against my pussy. I groaned, utterly at his mercy, no longer caring if he took his time or slammed into my fraught body.

It seemed slamming was on the agenda. In one hard, pumping thrust he buried it to the hilt, shoving in until his balls rammed against my spread ass. I cried out as my vaginal muscles spasmed in protest, pain and pleasure mixing in a confusing cocktail of bliss, sweet flames licking me from the inside out.

"Fuck, you're so tight," he hissed, bending forward, shoving up my sweater and sucking my nipples through my thin bra.

I arched my back and flexed my neck. Hands still above my head, I gripped the sides of the bench. I was being impaled. It was agonizingly magnificent. Where his tongue had left off, his pubic bone took over, grinding and slamming onto my delicate, needy bud as he withdrew and then thrust back in. An orgasm was rushing to meet me with all the grace of a steam train, gripping my chest and somersaulting my stomach.

He shifted upright between my raised legs, the high bench an ideal height for him to stand tall whilst he fucked me. I watched his head tip back, his neck tendons thick like cords as a flash of lightning streaked overhead. He looked down at where we'd joined, wrapped his fingers around my bare hips and rammed me harder onto his concrete cock, watching the erotic action with blazing eyes.

I curled forward and gripped his wrists. He was filling me entirely; he was so deep I could feel him nudging my diaphragm, and my breaths had to hitch in time with his frantic thrusts. I tried to speak but couldn't form coherent words, and the sound emerged as a wail of pleasure.

He bent over me again, pressing me backward. "I'm gonna come. For Christ's sake, join me this time."

I didn't need to be asked, the orgasm was there for the taking. By bending forward, he'd shifted the folds of my sex and my clit was in maximum connection with his surging body. This, combined with the colossal dick stabbing my pussy, had me on my way to heaven.

I stopped kissing him, lost to everything but ecstasy; it

hovered, it flew and then crashed through me. I clenched his dick relentlessly, over and over, pulling him higher, squeezing him tighter.

He froze at the highest point and then pulsated wildly within me. "Fuck, yes," he groaned scooping his arms under my shoulders and pinning me to his chest in a viselike grip.

I opened my eyes, body trembling, insides convulsing and legs shaking in their suspended position.

He lifted his head and looked into my dazed eyes. A sheen of sweat sparkled on his brow. "That," he said breathlessly, a ghost of a smile dancing on his lips, "is my idea of body molding."

RAPTURE

Angela Caperton

There's nothing to do but wait," Robert said as they watched
the full moon rise.

"You think He's coming, Robert?" Margaret asked, her
voice softer than the October breeze that blew from the river
and tugged her long, brown hair.

"'Course He is. You remember what Brother William said.
'Today is the day of our deliverance.'"

Margaret shifted her weight carefully as she braced the low
heel of her shoe against a shingle's edge. Her flowing, white
woolen robe, which had clung so pleasantly in the afternoon,
now seemed insufficient against the chill of night. "I figured
He'd come in the daytime."

"No man can name the hour," Robert replied, his voice
starting out strong but ending soft. In the heat of day, he had
gathered his robe around his waist, but now he unrolled it over
his cotton trousers.

"But Brother William named the day," she said, carefully

tucking her legs under her. "The day's over, Robert, and here we are."

Robert turned toward her, the last purple of twilight shining in the black thatch of his rough-cut hair. In the deepening shadows she could not see his eyes, but she knew the look that would be in them, an expression of earnest innocence that melted her heart.

She had studied his eyes all day, since their early morning ascent to the high roof. Now in the shadows, she thought again of when she first saw the light in them—at the meeting in late summer. In Dutch Cooper's field, the withering heat of that August night nearly melted bodies together, but by lantern light, in the eighteen hundred and forty-fourth year of the millennium, Brother William brought the word of God to Samuel's Ferry, and everyone witnessed that Rapture was at hand.

"And the chosen will be taken up," the gray giant preached, his voice like thin thunder, reedy with age but strong as his faith. "The day has been given to me and those who will be saved shall know the truth when they shall hear it, and he who does not hear shall be destroyed!"

Margaret's heart raced when his voice rose, as the congregation cried their joy, and in a proclamation Margaret knew to be God's own, Brother William shared with them—with the residents of Samuel's Ferry!—the time of God's coming. Margaret barely drew breath. She'd live to see Him! She'd be one of the chosen, for she had heard Brother William's words! She had been chosen and nothing, nothing could make her feel more worthy, more blessed.

Robert had been on the bench beside her. His hand had slipped into hers, warm and alive, the pads a little rough, but not unpleasant. His thumb stroked the back of her hand, and little ripples of pleasure stitched their way across her arms and into her breasts. She had looked at their joined hands and then into his face, the deep-water blue of his eyes, his dark hair raggedly shorn, but intriguingly complementary to the strong angles of his smiling face. He wore brown trousers and his thin shirt was clean except for the wet stains at his armpits, but Margaret couldn't hold that against him. Every man and woman in the field had those stains. She smiled at him, grinning foolishly. Her breasts ached and her cheeks burned a moment, then she looked away from the stranger beside her and back at Brother William, his every word a ringing revelation.

She had been chosen. And she'd never felt more alive.

That had been eight weeks ago and since then most of the brothers and sisters who had been at the meeting in Dutch Cooper's field fell back into their sinful ways, only a few remaining faithful to mark the passage of days through summer fire and into the misty days of autumn.

The dozen remaining faithful had gathered one October morning on the edge of town and walked in robed procession to the old Hathorne house on a hill overlooking the ferry.

Three stories high and sturdily decrepit, the house had been untenanted for a generation, and no one stopped the congregation's resolute march, though several townsfolk gathered to mock.

Solemnly, the faithful had climbed a rickety ladder to the first floor balcony and then made their way with rope and a pulley set by Robert and Mr. Wright to the very highest peak of the roof, which they had quickly discovered was too precarious a perch. Over the course of the morning, they had settled in couples and trios on the gable roofs of the second floor, perching like enormous white doves on the splintering shingles.

By noon, the mockers had grown tired and gone back to town, and by the middle of the afternoon, the faithful had begun to grumble. By ones and twos that had made their way down the rope, until only Robert, Margaret, and the Wrights remained. Then Mrs. Wright had grown worried about the children and, in the first moments of red sunset, Robert had helped the family down the rope, and they had departed with a promise to return at the first sound of thunder or trumpets.

"You reckon there will be fire?" Robert asked her.

"We'll be taken up before the fire comes," she said.

He smiled at her. "Fire'd almost feel good."

"Robert!" she gasped, but, in spite of her shock at his blasphemy, she giggled. The tickle of laughter overwhelmed her and she saw Robert stiffen. He looked down at himself, at the white robe he wore, and his chest began to rise and fall. His eyes grew wide and then he too burst out in a deep chuckle that merged with her laughter and it echoed along the riverbanks, the only possible response to the madness of the day.

"We are a pair, aren't we, Margaret?" Robert slowly regained his breath, and she heard concern in his voice. "We should've climbed down with the others. Now we'll break our necks if we try or we'll freeze if we stay!"

She moved closer to him, put her hand on his arm. "We'll stay," she said. "But we won't freeze."

She held his arm close against her, wedging it between her smocked breasts, thrilling at the beat of her heart against his strength and warmth. His breath steamed her forehead and made her smile. It would grow colder soon—if the eternal flames of damnation didn't descend upon the earth and burn the unbelievers to ashes, the Wrights included. Still, she could think of no place on earth she would rather be than here, with Robert, even if the fires burned her, too.

The comfortable silence that fell between them dragged on until the last glimmer of dusk was swallowed by the night. The moon watched unashamed, and Margaret wondered what would happen to it when He came. Would it still be there, or would its wicked pull and maddening shine be cast out of the sky? She hoped not. She'd always liked the moon, liked how its light felt on her skin, how it seemed to turn her to warm mist, and sometimes, when she'd stared at it on long summer nights, she felt its touch in her most private parts. She never told anyone about the odd tightness in her center or the warm wetness between her legs, but she wanted to tell Robert now.

"Sh-should we pray, Robert?" He shifted some, wrapping his arms around her and pulling her closer to him as he braced his feet to hold them in the narrow valley where the gable and the roof met.

"Quietly, I guess. Wouldn't want to wake the neighbors." The laughter came again, not so deep nor so long, and they grew quiet, lying face-to-face, close enough now for her to see his eyes, like lakes with the rising moon reflected.

He leaned close and whispered against her ear, his lips warm. "Our Father, who art..."

Margaret closed her eyes and echoed his words in hushed whispers. She felt the feather of his breath on her cheek, and then their noses bumped, and she felt his breath on her lips, the prayers almost silent, because her breath was gone.

Her heart pounded as Robert's mouth closed over hers, firm, moist; he pressed against her, not the chaste peck of Brother and Sister, but a kiss....

Her lips parted, welcoming him, her arms circling him as she felt the first delicious stroke of his tongue along hers. A giddy feeling bolted through her and for a moment, she knew the sense of certain damnation.

Then her arms wrapped around his chest, her fingers grew lost in his hair, and a groan of desire, the most joyous "Amen"

Margaret had ever heard, filled her ears.

His hands found her breast under the thin Ascension robe and the shift she wore beneath it. Wetness returned between her legs, along with surging heat and as the moon glittered in the sky, Margaret felt herself under its spell.

She pressed hard against him, their robes tangling. His hands caressed her back, one slipping down over her bottom, impatient with the pale wool. The heat of his palm burned through her linen shift as he worked the dress up her calf, then her thigh. The kiss never relaxed, never ceased to demand and give.

His hellfire hand ran up the bare skin of her leg, lingering at the knee, then climbing, fast and certain, up her thigh to the place no man had ever touched before, but where she had stroked sometimes on the most lunatic of nights.

Her breath disappeared. When his fingers found the wetness between her legs, she gasped and bit him in her shock, tasting the blood on his lips. He did not seem to feel it, the eternal kiss breaking only for a moment, then continuing, slippery and salty and even more fevered than before.

His finger entered her, parting the folds easily, and he pushed, sliding in and out slowly, spreading the wetness, smearing it. *Damnation*, she thought, but she bent her leg, opening wider to let him in.

He broke the kiss and she lunged at him, caught his jaw between her teeth, clenched a moment and then kissed upward, nuzzling his ear, while his hand continued its slow assault, parting the folds, playing at the secret center of her pleasure until a tide washed over her. She shivered and bucked slowly against him, astonished that any touch should feel so good and that a man might know the manner to bring about such ecstasy.

Margaret cried out, and the moon spun in heaven.

She saw it then, His gift. The perfect beauty of the sky, the silver circle, the shattered crystalline splendor of the stars; the whispering wind, its breath cool on her bare, wet thigh; this pleasure.

This love.

Trembling, she turned, moving against him, her robe an impediment now. She cast it away, only the shift between her and the sacred night, and she reached under his robe. His hands played on her arms and shoulders, and she felt the heat of his gaze, though his face lay in shadows.

She heard the whisper of his hastened breath like a new hymn.

The buttons of his trousers were big and easily undone, the pants joining their robes. His fingers worked the buttons of his shirt quickly, opening the front, exposing his chest. Margaret had never seen a man unclothed before, but Mrs. Wright had told her men's members were much the same as a horse preparing to mount a mare.

She wondered for a moment if the miracle at her fingertips was the right thing, for it was nothing like a horse's member. Robert's was pale as parchment in the moonlight, softer than a velvet hat, and warm as an ember, hardening even as she freed it, though it was very hard already.

She felt no shame, no sin, only a filling of her heart that blossomed through every cell of her body and a pool of heavy liquid heat between her legs.

Her fingers traced the soft ridge of a vein, following it from the stiff curly hair, up the shaft to a line of wrinkled skin and the satin-soft edge of the emergent, bulbous tip.

"Margaret," Robert groaned, his head thumping back against the shingles.

She sat up and peered down at the hard flesh in her hand. In a shining ray of moonlight, glistening on top, a shimmering drop crowned its glory. Margaret reached out, rubbed the moist gem between thumb and forefinger, and then brought it to her lips. She touched her finger to her tongue, as she might taste a mysterious kitchen spill to determine salt or sugar. The tang of it shocked her, and following a whim, she lowered her head and reached out to the slick, moonlit plum with her lips and the tip of her tongue.

Robert's head fell against the roof again, and the loud rap brought Margaret's attention back from her exploration.

"Robert, are you all right?"

He sat up beside her and stared for only a moment. With smooth grace, he caught the edge of her shift in his hands, pulled it over her head and exposed her to the night. The air's chill evaporated as Robert pulled her hard against him. He rolled carefully, his bare legs and chest blanketing her, his kiss long and deep, his tongue delving as if he sought her soul, stroking, coaxing, beseeching. Her arms encircled him under his shirt, fingers thrilling at his skin and the hard muscles beneath. She returned his kiss with equal fire, knowing their path had but one destination.

Heaven.

He lowered his head and took the tip of her breast between his lips. A sigh rose in her throat, but she clamped her lips against its release. She gripped his head, gently holding while his tongue tortured her with small, whipping circles around the taut flesh. The hard length of his cock pressed against her thigh, the dewy head making a sticky ring to bind them together. His hands roamed over her, stroking, exploring, testing and tempting. Her skin became less than mist between them. She felt every stroke, every nip, every kiss in her blood. When his fingers returned to the wet folds, she arched her hips against them, entreating, praying for their judgment with every squirm, every writhe. Two fingers slipped easily into the chalice, wet with her wine; such miraculous fingers, such knowing. He found the button, tested the hardness of it, the sensitized flesh a gate to paradise. He stroked, teased, coaxed, until Margaret saw again the promised land of blinding light, but then Robert stopped.

She whimpered—a starving soul denied bread—and clutched at him as if he were all that buoyed her from drowning.

His warm breath licked her ear, "Margaret, I love you." He moved fully over her, his legs and hips between hers. The hard length of his cock pulled sticky from her thigh, breaking the slick suction it had formed there. For a moment, panic filled her. Was he leaving her?

Then the cushioned rock of his prick pushed along the line of her sex, worshipping the gate before pressing, sure and steady, beyond the threshold.

Brilliant ripples of pleasure shot through her as he pushed the bulbed head into her.

Into her.

Her legs wrapped around him, enfolding his body in welcome as he paused just within. Margaret knew there was more room. She remembered his fingers and her own, and she wanted him all the way in.

Robert's breath hissed in harsh rasps. She cupped his face in her hands and drew him to her. Her lips met his and melded them together, a bridge between their souls. Her tongue tangled joyfully with his in the ethereal place that was neither him nor her. And with a commanding pin of her tongue beneath his, Robert's weight settled upon her and his long, hard cock slid like silk deep within her, deeper than fingers had ever been.

A sharp rending pain shot through her, but the pain dulled in the fullness of Robert's motion, slow at first, careful not to hurt her, then quickening, slippery and ever deeper.

She thought of hymns, of the pulse of the pianos she'd heard in church. Steady, true, the bass chords that kept the time of the song. Robert's hips moved against her, sliding his cock into her, pulling it back until it almost left her completely. She felt every stroke, the steady fullness inside her, then the nearly heart-breaking removal of his flesh. She kissed him, landing her praise and her thanks upon whatever skin met her mouth—shoulders, neck, lips, cheek. His breath puffed like a running stallion's as he thrust into her, long and vital, his desire for her manifest in each tensing of his buttocks, each grind of his hips.

At each stroke, each inner caress, Margaret's flesh expanded, flourished. A sensation grew within her, a sister to her earlier bliss, but more intense, more divine.

He pulled away from her, but stayed fused to her hips, his cock a stake within the ground of her body. He carefully settled upon his knees, his toes against the edge of the roof. He gripped her hips and pulled her even more tightly against his own, then drove into her again, finding her center with the precision of a smith striking an edge. She arched against the shock and gasped as his fingers found the button and manipulated it as he slid in and out of her.

Her eyes closed as her spirit and mind sang with the sensations of her body. Each satin-hard invasion pushed her closer to transcendence.

Her muscles tightened around his cock, and Robert's breath expelled in a cracked growl. He thrust hard, a tremor of enchanting pain pushing a cry from her lips. He stayed there, completely buried, flushed and heavy, inside her.

"Sweet Jesus, Margaret," Robert whispered before he withdrew, slow, almost fully, then slid into her again, harder, the rhythm urgent, flashing, as if he might die before reaching the finish. And all the while, his thumb played at the swollen button and drowned Margaret with sensation, jarring, frenzied, wild until the slick pumping turned her visions to gold and the moon above became nothing but a pale cousin to the ecstasy that exploded through her body.

She cried out, singing her joy to Robert, to the stars. Overwhelming pleasure engulfed her, braised her, burned her to cinders in rippling waves of blissful heat.

He thrust twice more, his breath so ragged Margaret worried after his health as his weight pushed her against the roof and she overflowed; a warm, thick trickle of his spend leaked out and quickly cooled against her buttocks.

She opened her eyes and looked up at the moon, smiling, awestruck at how beautiful she felt.

How divine.

They did not sleep, but made love twice more before the dawn. When the morning's red light cast the shadow of the Hathorne house in long black ripples on the rolling edge of the river, they sat up, and watched the world turn golden.

Naked they were, like Adam and Eve, awake in the new day, and a weary reluctance touched her heart as she slipped on her shift and folded the Ascension robe. She would not wear it again.

Robert eased on his trousers, and she sighed as she watched his miraculous cock, the rod of his dominion, vanish beneath the coarse cotton.

Her eyes met his and she saw there all the things she felt in her own heart. No disappointment at all, no regret.

Only rapture.

BELTED

Rachel Kramer Bussel

You'd never know the belt is there by looking at him. It's lost between his shirt and his pants, tucked away, hidden, pulled close, serving a dual purpose. You'd never know it's there, unless he made a point of showing you. And he does, often, a hand resting there as a reminder in public, an intimation of what will happen in private. You have no idea how many other girls he makes a point of showing it to, but the reason you keep returning is that when you're with him, you don't care about the other girls. There could be hundreds, thousands even; as long as he looks at you the way he does when he unbuckles and unfurls the soft, worn, brown leather, then coils the belt purposefully around his hand, you can let yourself believe he wears it just for you.

This isn't the first belt that's been used to strike you. There was the boyfriend in college who had you bend over, skirt around your ankles, camera flashing and belt lashing against your skin before plunging his oversized cock into your unprepared ass. He was all flash and no finesse.

Your lover is the opposite, or rather, flash and finesse mixed together in a dizzying way, with plenty of substance to back them up. He holds the belt like it belongs in his hand, like it's an extension of him. He tells you that he thinks about you every day when he loops it through his pants, when he touches the cool metal buckle. Alone in some room or another—never either of your bedrooms—your body reacts before you have time to consider its wisdom when you see him reaching for the buckle. After all, you know from experience that could mean anything—he's giving you his cock to suck, he's going to shackle your arms behind your back, he's going to pull your hair hard and slap your face until you cry, he's going to beat you until your skin is heated from the outside in. All of these are possibilities, and all of these bring you pleasure, but you hope it's the latter.

The belt is able to speak in ways that even the both of you, wordsmiths by trade, cannot always do. The belt is not a "toy" for "foreplay" but a separate part of your sex life, one that may appear at any moment. Its presence lurks while you casually sip your drinks at the bar, hidden but powerful; your fingers are itching to stroke it, if only so they can be slapped away. You never know if he will bring it out, how he will use it, how much of the belt and himself he will give you.

You try not to be greedy, but you hope it'll be a moment like this: You're sore from having his cock inside you, from him holding you down, from his hand crushing your neck. Sore in a good way, so you almost don't even miss the belt—almost. You never have much time, can never stay overnight, have to steal hours out of other people's schedules to accommodate this affair, so you learn to take what you can get. You're wondering when he will have to leave, when this spell of lust will fade back into real life, when he reaches for the belt from the floor. "Turn over," he tells you, and you roll onto your stomach, your pale backside before him.

Your face is turned away from him, sunken into the softness of the pillow, freshly washed hair now tousled and messy. The tip of the belt rests against your newly shaved lips as you hear the words, "Spread your legs." You do, because you always do, because this is what your relationship is about: he orders, you obey, and you both like it like that. Your hands instinctively curl around the pillow, long nails digging into the cotton and feathers as you wait. The belt strikes the air and you shiver, feeling a breeze that may be a phantom one or may be very, very real. The next sound you hear coincides with a strike of the belt on your cheeks, both of them, a slice that takes a moment to process before you say the words almost automatically: "Thank you."

There's never a "You're welcome," or rather, not a verbal one. It's implied by the next stinging strike, by the fact that you're deemed worthy at all. He doesn't talk then, is almost solemn as you wait for it to be over with equal parts dread and glee.

But those kinds of smacks aren't what make you come. No, that's saved for when he makes you cry. You turn over and open your eyes for a moment to look at him, hovering over you. You marvel that you can feel so close when he's not touching you with his body at all. The belt is capable of magic. You start to shiver once you realize what's going to happen, that the belt is not just teasing your lips with a kiss, though you pucker up when it approaches.

Then the belt moves on to its real work, kissing your other set of lips harder, the equivalent of a shove-you-against-the-wall, bruising kiss. This kiss is merely an introduction, a warm-up. You know what's coming and even though you want it, you press your legs together involuntarily until he barks at you to put them back. You shut your eyes because you know you can't watch this. Your hands are twisted above your head, clinging to each other for some kinky version of safety. You focus on keeping your legs open, all of you exposed. When the belt strikes there, right there, you don't quite scream; it's more of a strangled, garbled cry. Your hand automatically goes to cover the sting, to cradle yourself. You finally get a "Good girl."

You try to turn over, to curl into a ball, but you're not allowed, or rather, your desire to prove yourself wins out over your desire to stop what's coming. You didn't travel for hours just to shy away from the pain. But you almost forget that when the next blow strikes. You wonder how the tender skin between your legs can stand that force, and then you stop wondering when the belt moves upward, to your breasts, your pebbled nipples no match for the blows. You arch your back and thrust upward, even though inside, you want to cower. You reluctantly remember telling him you wanted bruises there, marks you could proudly reveal with a hint of cleavage, a well-timed reveal as you lean over on the train. You still want the marks but breathe deep through your nose, twist your fingers more tightly around each other, to get through them. You bite your lip as the sweet pain of the belt heats your chest and wanders downward. You almost get used to the rhythm, your nipples stubbornly rising after each blow.

Then it's back down, back to the place that no longer feels like your cunt, not the way it's being set afire again and again. These lashes aren't as swift as the ones against your breasts, but they are sure, steady. He's not twice your size for no reason, and each slap strikes precisely where he wants it to. The tears finally appear in the form of sobs, traveling fast through your body, a current of energy you use to sustain yourself through the last few lashes. You'd think the pain would be a little more subdued, the pussy's diminishing law of returns, but no. You feel every

ounce of force he uses for each stroke, every bite of the leather
into your inner thighs, against your wetness. You have a vision
of the belt wrapped around your throat, the buckle cold against
your skin as you stare deep into his eyes, but that was another
time, another place. The next blow has you thrashing so much
he has to hold you down.

Is it the belt that makes you come? The leather, the thrash,
the pain, the jolt? Is it the force behind it? Is it the noises he
makes as he does it, the hitches of breath that are nothing like
your shuddering sobs but are music to your ears nonetheless—is
that what makes you finally go over the edge? Is it him holding
you down, him promising you pain that may or may not come?

Maybe it's all of it, all the forces combining to make the
orgasm nothing like what you were expecting, the kind where
your body bonds with the belt, giving back some of its life force,
only to have it beaten back into you. Though you know that logi-
cally, rationally, it's impossible, you hope the belt has absorbed
some of your tears, has taken them and held on to them for
next time, has put the pain that you mostly wanted, but kind of
didn't, somewhere for safekeeping, somewhere he can hold next
to his skin any time he desires.

Oh, it's not like you really have time to think all that or think
anything, not then. The belt is reminding you, lash by lash, that
you must stay open, stay ready, stay through the moments when
you don't know how you will get through it, stay through the
times you don't have a chance to take a bracing breath or perform
any other magic tricks to turn the pain into something else. By
now even the light touches, the strokes of the belt's rough edge
against your fleshy inner thigh, the dance of the musky leather
against your cheek, are enough to make you shudder, like when
he raises his hand to smack you but stops right before his fingers
reach the finish line. The effect is the same.

You breathe through your nose, a more refined type of breath, one granted you by the momentary lapse before the belt is between your legs again, crashing hard, calling forth wetness you didn't know you still had. Pain, pleasure, obedience, pride, love, hate, fear ride each other along the waves of your body until you hardly know who you are anymore. You've moved beyond some simple goal of taking it into somewhere else, somewhere you're afraid to look at too closely lest it prove to be just a mirage.

And then, almost too fast, it's over. The belt lies limp on the bed and you're allowed to press your legs together again, to admire the bruises on your chest that you will wind up keeping close like a secret. You wipe the tears from your cheeks, embarrassed but secretly pleased. What happens after that hardly even matters, because that is what will remain, not the belt or the pain or the marks, but the beauty of being transformed by each of them into someone new, blossoming like the bruises on and under your skin; traveling with him somewhere far away, somewhere magical no one else will ever visit, where each strike of the belt serves to bind you together in this sensual cocoon, sealing you in with its heat long after the physical marks drift away.

You hope it'll be something like that, but with him, you never know what you're going to get, and you wouldn't have it any other way.

RISE AND SHINE

Heidi Champa

My dress was fierce and so were my shoes. The red carpet passed by in a breeze, with cameras flashing all around me. Everyone asked who I was wearing and if I thought I had a chance of winning. I tried to savor the moments, but they all seemed to go by in a blur. Before I knew it, I was sitting in the velvet seat, waiting to hear my name being called by last year's winner. Suddenly, everything seemed to slow down, the room and all its movement seemed to come to a stop. The only thing I could hear was the hiss of the microphone, before I heard my name echoing off the walls. I won. I actually won. I barely felt my feet as I moved to the front, walking on a cloud up the stairs to the wide, golden stage. With the trophy pressed into my hands, I turned to face my adoring public.

The haze of spotlights made it hard to see the crowd, but across the buzzing room, I could just make out the faces of all my fellow actors honoring me. The award felt heavy and warm in my hands. The tears that pricked the corners of my eyes started to fall gently at first, then steadier. The moment was just sinking in, when I felt a finger skim over my pussy lips. I looked over my shoulder at Russell Crowe and the trophy lady. They were too far away to be touching me—a shame, too, as the three of us could have had a good time together. No, this hand seemed to be coming from nowhere, but it felt so real.

In an instant, I realized it was real. My award was the fake. The dream that had carried me away was fading and weakening at the edges. My head was cloudy, sleepy. The hand between my legs was getting through the dreamscape. A mouth on my neck was the next sensation to push through the barrier, blurring the lines of fantasy and reality. The soft lips sweeping from my ear to my collarbone were making it hard to finish my acceptance speech. The room seemed to be getting smaller, the lights a lot less bright. A pinch of teeth on my soft flesh made me wince, but I kept on going.

A light fingertip brush against my clit aroused a gasp from the crowd, as I tried to continue with my thank-you list. Soon the crowd had disappeared altogether. I tried to open my eyes, but they wouldn't budge. Fingers spread my cunt lips apart, but my mind still groped for some sense of what was really going on. Was it coming from my head or next to me in the bed? When a finger entered my moistening slit, I told my body to move. Nothing happened. I felt heavy, as if trapped underwater. Thoughts came from my brain, moving at slow-motion pace. My body was ignoring my orders. The only thing that was getting through was the steady plunge of the finger entering my pussy. Another finger moved inside, filling me. Slowly, my head began to grasp what was occurring. My body was still uncooperative, leaving me defenseless against the invading, slippery digits.

The sensations of heat and pleasure rolled through me, washing over me like a warm bath. Again, I tried to move, tried to engage with the real world. I was trapped in between waking and sleep, unable to get any closer to either one. My pussy was filled and aching, drowning out all the other efforts I was making. Fighting a losing battle, I let go of everything.

My nipple started to ache and tighten; a burst of pain followed the gentle tease of pleasure. Another hand was groping me through my tank top. Then the sensation became hot, wet, but my eyes refused my repeated requests to open and reveal my torturer. The heat moved away, finding my other nipple alone and unattended. It was then I smelled the sweet tones of his shampoo. The sound of his mouth sucking my nipple was seeping into my hazy subconscious. I could feel reality coming in, my body slowly rousing awake. I wanted to stay in the ether, where I could just feel and not think. The wetness seeping between my thighs and his persistent mouth were making that difficult. My body was waking up first; my mind was slowly following behind.

His thumb strummed at my clit, his tongue moved off my nipples. They sat hard, aching for a squeeze. I felt my mouth open, but my eyes were still being stubborn. My body lay limp, the safe cover of the blanket gone. For a moment or two, the sensations were all over my body, a blurred, warm feeling, my mind having no idea where it was coming from or where it was going—until I felt a hot rush sweeping over my pussy. It was just like the feeling my nipples had been having a few minutes before. I knew it must be his tongue on my cunt. He picked up the same relentless rhythm on my clit, his fingers back inside me with their gentle twist and pull.

I left my eyes closed, trying in vain to hold on to the last moments of oblivion. My body was starting to respond without me, rolling my hips into his mouth, urging his tongue along. My thighs spread wider, opening me up to his demanding mouth.

Three fingers were thrusting inside me, bringing me little by little into the waking world. For the first time, I allowed a moan to escape my mouth. I could hear him groaning as he stroked me; it sounded far away, but I could feel it vibrating against my skin. I still didn't open my eyes to see him. He left my clit, and I moaned my disappointment until I felt the wet trail of his tongue tease down to my puckered ass. I felt the pointed tip slip gently around my asshole, rimming me until I was sorely tempted to open my eyes.

I didn't. I knew he was trying to wake me up, but I was trying to stay in that beautiful fog a little bit longer. Undeterred, he went back to licking my hard clit, leaving a wet finger teasing my ass. I felt the concentrated pressure of him pushing my ass open. I was so relaxed; he was inside me with so little effort. His fingers filled me up, leaving my pussy and ass open and stretched. I kept my eyes closed, still trying to revel in the thick-as-honey feeling of sleep mixed with ecstasy. While his finger wiggled inside my ass, he sucked my clit hard. Another moan broke from my lips, my hips again moving under his tongue. Faster, then slower, his pace was erratic, making me buck off the warm flannel sheets. My eyes stayed locked tight. I knew I wasn't fooling him, or myself, but I wanted to hang on to those last gauzy soft moments before I gave in to the sharp edge of orgasm that was heading toward me.

Then, suddenly, everything stopped. His mouth was gone, his fingers leaving me empty and wanting. Desperate as I was to open my eyes, to see what he was doing, I didn't. I squeezed them shut, waiting and panting on the bed. He covered me, his whole body pressing into me. My legs went instinctively around his back. I felt his mouth on mine, his tongue salty with my taste. His cock was nudging at my wet cunt, sliding and slipping over my clit as he adjusted his position over me. I pushed my hips up into him, but he wouldn't fit inside.

"Come on, open your eyes. It's time to wake up."

His breath was hot on my ear, but not as hot as the tongue sliding over my earlobe. With it caught between his teeth, he pulled at my skin, urging me to finally look at him. I moaned but kept my eyes shut. I wanted just a few more moments. I wasn't ready to wake up yet. His teeth sank into my neck, a sucking bite a bit lower, a bit harder. My hands dug into the hard muscle of his shoulders, my nipples tightening against his chest.

"I won't fuck you until you open your eyes."

He moaned the ultimatum into my mouth, before plunging his tongue back inside. I made one last effort to ease his cock inside me, but he remained elusive. He had left me no choice but to abandon the misty miasma and join the real world. I let my eyelids flutter open, seeing his straining blue eyes above me for the first time.

"Good morning."

The words left his throat in a gasp as he slid inside me. I clutched around his cock, my pussy desperate to be filled after his fingers had left me. I was finally awake, finally able to see him. His mouth closed around my nipple, the feeling so much more intense than it had been a few moments ago. His cock moved inside me at the same slow pace as his mouth pulling on my rigid flesh.

"You interrupted a really good dream."

He looked up at me and I could see the laughter behind his eyes. Pinning my arms above my head, he thrust harder, grinding against my clit before pulling almost all the way out of me. Settling himself back inside me to the hilt, his eyes never left mine.

"I'm so sorry. How thoughtless of me."

His hands clasped mine, pressing me harder into the bed. I

could barely move beneath him; he was controlling everything. I needed to come; it felt like I'd been on the verge forever. But he kept me there, not letting me get any closer to what I wanted, what I needed.

"What was your dream about? Me?"

He thrust his cock deeper inside me, releasing my hands to push my legs higher and wider. I clung to his arms, trying to hold on as he fucked me harder.

"Not at first, but you kind of took over."

He couldn't help but laugh as he rubbed his hand down my trembling leg. I didn't know how much more I could take of his slow, deep fucking. I really needed to come.

"That sounds like me."

His mouth crushed mine with another destroying kiss. Rolling onto his back, he stayed inside me until I was straddling him, his hands steadying my hips. I rocked back, feeling every inch of him inside me, filling me completely. I rode him, my legs still heavy and tired from sleep. He lazily traced the skin of my stomach, avoiding the places I really wanted him to touch me. I could feel my nipples harden painfully as my orgasm remained too far away. The ache behind my clit was becoming a huge fire of need. I was desperate for him to touch me, to touch the swollen nub of my clit.

As if reading my mind, he dragged his thumb over my clit; the slow circle broke through the last wall keeping back my impending orgasm. He had to hold me up as I came. Shuddering and writhing on top of him, my strength was sapped by every ripple coursing through my body. Everything started to break apart, my mind smashed to bits as my body tightened repeatedly. My pussy started to quake, pleasure bordering on pain shooting all through my body. I felt like I was being pulled apart by the joy of it all, his cock drawing every last ounce of feeling out of my body. I couldn't think or breathe. All I could do was come. I could hardly believe it was real. It felt better than any dream I'd ever had.

Collapsing on his chest, I felt him thrust up harder into my pussy as his own orgasm hit. I lay there helpless and spent as he came inside me, too tired to do anything but take him. Soon, he too was exhausted, limp and satisfied beneath me. He moved first, rolling me off his sweaty body. He pushed my crazy morning hair aside and kissed my sleepy mouth.

"Sorry I woke you?"

His boyish grin gave me the strength to wrap myself around him and cover us with the mess of blankets we'd created.

"Not a chance."

TAKING THE REINS

Vanessa Vaughn

The boys don't understand. Not really.

I know for a fact that Jon doesn't love it the way I do.

As I straddle the seat and slowly lower myself down, I feel a familiar tingle of excitement deep inside. I can sense the monstrous size of the body between my thighs, the large chest expanding and contracting broadly with each breath. The smell of fresh, conditioned leather smothers my senses—well, that, and also the slight musky tinge of sweat. It is a raw smell mixed with rich, dark dirt.

It has become impossible for me to separate the scents of this place from the anticipation twisting inside me. They are connected. Now, the sights and sounds of one inevitably trigger the other. Just a glimpse of a dusty black velvet helmet, or of fingers clenched between thin leather gloves, makes my breath quicken. Then again, just the smallest peek at a man's muscled shoulder or of his rippled abs makes my thoughts turn to this, to the curve of a thoroughbred's slender neck or the solid bulge of a horse's muscular chest.

A slight hint of alcohol hangs in the air today, high above the other smells—no doubt from the metal cleaner I used on some of the tack. My spurs jingle a little as I slide my toes up against the stirrups.

I picture for a moment these metal rings hanging loose at Jon's thighs, banging lightly against his own thinner skin as I push the balls of my feet through and test them with my weight. But of course that is not what is happening. He would never allow a thing like that. My legs are wrapped tightly around a real stallion now. My shins are encased in a sheath of black leather, supple custom riding boots that stretch all the way up to my knees, shining with a high gloss. I slide them into the bell-shaped stirrups and push my heels down.

Pressing lightly, I feel my body align, my rump tightening and tilting my pelvis forward. I am in position, perfectly at attention with my lower back arched just enough. I can feel my clit pushing perfectly against the smooth rise of my saddle, the power of the huge animal beneath me as it shifts its weight, tensing between my legs.

Just the act of straddling something, anything, in public like this lends me a private thrill. And I feel a pleasure almost like exhibitionism in being able to parade such fetishistic gear— harnesses, whips, ropes, leather boots—openly in public without question.

I sometimes wonder if anyone else can sense what I feel when I am in the ring. Do they detect an unusual eagerness in me as I lead my animal out of the barn, as I slow him to a halt and mount him quickly? Can they see my cheeks, just a little more flushed than the other girls' as I ride?

On any given day, I can usually see one or two men here. They enjoy the surroundings, I'm sure—after all, there is certainly no shortage of beautiful women in this place. But, I wonder, do any of them closely watch my horse straining under me as I ride? Do any of them secretly wish they could take its place?

A mare nearby stomps her forefoot in the dirt of the covered arena and swishes her tail. At that, I tap my heels against my horse and click my tongue against my teeth. I feel the giant beneath me sway to life. I readjust my grip, my forearms precisely in line with the straps, and settle in to the comforting motion of his slow walk.

Jon never starts slow like this for me, never eases me into things the way I would if I had the reins. But here in the ring, I get to be on top for once. I feel the slow gait of the animal beneath me warming his limbs up gently, and I enjoy it. I enjoy knowing that my mount feels the anticipation just as I do. My horse knows there is a hard ride ahead, but he also knows that in the end he will be put away by his mistress, exhausted but satisfied. Why can Jon not see how wonderful that could feel?

Feeling frustrated, I kick my heels into the beast's side again. I feel his muscles tense, suddenly alert, as he quickens his pace into a trot. For a moment, I bounce in the saddle. I feel the most sensitive of areas between my legs being pounded against roughly as I am pulled slightly away from the saddle and then driven home again several times. I feel my body warming, the blood pulsing there and making my thoughts turn to one thing and one thing only: sex.

This makes me ache. But at the same time, I love it. Right now, I want to be fucked. I want *to* fuck. I feel like a schoolgirl who has just had her skirt lifted up and her bottom spanked savagely. I feel my face flush from the intimate strikes I am enduring.

But really, this is not just something I am tolerating. This is something I am demanding for myself. I am in full control of the horse's speed, of my contact with the saddle. At any time, I can stop the intensity of this. Perhaps that is why I feel so comfortable letting it happen.

I don't want what I'm feeling to be too obvious, though, and so I start to post. I rise up into a half-standing position with every step the horse takes, and then lower myself back down. Sadly, the feeling is much less intense. I feel naked suddenly without the constant violent sensation. But what I feel now is different. It is not as overwhelming but is much more precise.

Each time I lower myself, I touch the saddle lightly, softly squeezing my clit against the soft leather ridge in front of me. I feel less of that primal pull I felt before, but I also feel more in control. Posting, I pull my mount's head up and my body erect. I can feel the bit locking between his teeth and can see his ears turn slightly, poised and waiting for my next command.

Each soft stroke against the saddle turns me on incredibly, feeling gentle and rhythmic, almost like a leather paddle or a wide, fleshy dildo being rubbed against my pinkest, most tender folds.

My mount is impatient. I can sense that. He is eager to break into a run, to test his limits, to push himself; but I am able to hold him back. It seems incredible to me that I can stop him at all, that I can keep this beast from doing any of the things it wants. Yet I do. Here I am the master and he is just a tool, a means to an end, and I am the one that matters for once.

It is time, though, and we both know it. As I squeeze my calves against his warm sides, clenching, I think of Jon again, of how good he would feel in place of this stallion. Would Jon listen to me, though? Would he respond to my soft kicks, to the bridle encouraging him to lock his eyes straight ahead and not glance back and challenge me? No, I don't think he would. But then again, I never would have believed a large animal like this one could ever be made to follow my subtle suggestions, either.

If a high-spirited, one thousand pound horse could be trained, why not a willful man like Jon?

We break into a fast canter then, an all-out gallop being impossible in an enclosure, even in a ring as large as this. There can be no posting now, not at this pace. I feel his every tense muscle, every strike of his hoofs in the dirt as he propels me forward with those powerful haunches and rippling shoulders. Instead of rising up, now I use my entire body to press down, down against the saddle, down against the horse's back, down into the animal itself. I feel my pulse pounding in my ears, faster and more deafening all the time. I feel this same throb at other times, too, nights when Jon is behind me and I am on my knees, nights when I feel his huge hands at my waist, his thick cock pushing its way inside.

And now I ride my mount with that same zeal. I love being ridden, used, taken. When I want sex, I always want it rough. But at times, I also want to take the reins. I want to be in charge of exactly what I feel and when. I want to make demands of my own.

I picture Jon wearing this saddle now and not the horse, my crop landing across his backside with a sharp crack as he flinches and sucks in a shocked breath. I picture the bit stretching the corners of his mouth, the girth secured by my expert hands, gripping his waist tightly and even uncomfortably.

The scene shifts in my mind, suddenly, unbidden, the way that fantasies do. I am still the rider, but now Jon is lying on his back. I can feel that massive cock of his poised under me like a thick coil of rope. He trembles as I slap him again—with my palm this time, not the whip. He closes his eyes and I start to lower myself onto him. I breathe slowly and feel myself stretched wide.

My pussy is throbbing now as I grind it into the saddle. I exaggerate the horse's canter, urging him forward aggressively with my hips. I feel the sheen of sweat on my brow, the velvety helmet tight against my forehead.

The longing between my legs has quickened into a pulse, and now I can feel I am on the verge of something. I squeeze my thighs against the struggling horse and push my breeches hard into the leather and finally feel it, finally feel that primal sensation I have been struggling for.

It does not wash over me, though. This escapes, like an animal released from a cage. My body had been tense, expectant, like a racehorse shifting behind a starting block. This feeling is the opening of those racing gates, adrenaline pumping through my body and spurring it on. The rumbling between my legs is like the thunder of hooves. I shake with it, am deafened by it.

And then I think of Jon and clench my fingers tightly, reflexively, so that I don't drop the reins.

FIRST DATE WITH THE DOM

Noelle Keely

A hot summer day in Boston had morphed into a sultry night by the time Serena and Jack dragged themselves out of the Barking Crab. Still talking, they made their way across Fort Point Channel to South Station, where Serena would need to catch the T if she was heading home to Dorchester.

Then came the inevitable moment where they stood on the street and stared at each other, trying to figure out what to do next.

What they both wanted was obvious.

Serena could smell it over the combination of salt and exhaust fumes that scented the air this close to the harbor. She could taste it, as she could still taste Jack's fingers. She could feel it in her blood and bones as much as in her tight, sensitive nipples and wet, pulsing pussy.

Desire. Need. Want.

Hunger.

All the dark creatures that lived inside her brain clamored for their chance to come out to play: the broken virgin, the whore, the temple dancer, the pirate's captive, the French maid, the prisoner of the Inquisition.

And the slave, always the slave.

But she didn't dare to speak.

Odd, that. In the past, when she'd wanted a man anywhere as badly as she wanted Jack, she hadn't waited around for him to make a move. Oh, no, she'd made her dishonorable intentions clear.

But Jack froze that bold part of her, even while he melted the rest. Jack's pale, steady gaze and cool voice and the knowledge of what he was and the feeling that he wouldn't react well to being pushed, held her back.

So Serena bit her lip and waited.

For what must have only been about thirty seconds, but felt more like thirty minutes.

The hell with being decorous, she decided. If she was stepping out of line, he'd let her know. And with any luck, the way he let her know might be fun.

She stretched up, put her arms around Jack's neck and kissed him.

He didn't seem to mind, judging from the way he pulled her closer, the way he met her tongue with his and orchestrated their dance.

But he pulled away after a distressingly short time and looked down at her rather sternly. "Patience, pretty lady," he said, shaking his head. "I prefer to set the pace."

For a second, she thought she might have actually angered him. He seemed remote and somehow bigger: taller, broader, more menacing, almost frightening.

It was a type of frightening, though, that went straight to her groin, stabbing at her clit.

Then one of his hands buried itself in the thick curls at the back of her neck and pulled her head back. "Fortunately," he whispered, "you were only about two seconds ahead of me."

He kissed her.

Such simple words: she could tell her mother the next time they talked, "And then Jack kissed me," and her mother would say something along the lines of "How sweet!"

Sweet, though, had nothing to do with this devouring, possessive mouth, this fierce grip on her hair, this other hand firmly cupping her ass and pressing her pelvis against his body. Sweet had nothing to do with the conflagration roaring through her body, burning up her will to do anything for the moment but touch Jack, please Jack, be pleased by Jack. And "sweet" certainly had nothing to do with the hard cock pushing against her as if it could penetrate her through their clothes, there on the corner of Atlantic Avenue by South Station.

If it could, she'd let him.

As it was, she was going to take what she could get, here on the street. As long as he didn't mind, that is.

She moved experimentally against him, shifting so her clit, through the thin fabric of her dress and panties, was in contact with him. Then, thinking fast, she broke from the kiss just long enough to ask, "Is this all right?"

"Oh, yes," he whispered, his breath hot against her ear. "That's a good girl. See if you can make yourself come by rubbing yourself against me. I'll reward you if you can."

Oh, my god. If she'd been turned on before, she was about a hundred times more so now just by hearing him say these words.

It was early enough that the streets were still full, pedestrians stepping around the island they made in the sea of foot traffic, sometimes with an indulgent laugh, sometimes not. Some little piece of brain still grounded in the everyday world said she should be self-conscious, ashamed of such slutty behavior in public.

Serena told that little piece of brain to shut the hell up.

Serena ground against Jack, thrusting her pelvis wantonly against the bulge in his pants as they kissed.

Each movement sent little fingers of pleasure through her, reaching up to meet the pleasure flowing down from the lips Jack was still devouring. It was enough to feel amazing, but not enough to push her over the edge. She shifted, meaning to straddle his thigh—it was subtle as a ton of bricks falling on your head, but maybe any gawking passersby would be having extrahot evenings themselves—but Jack put both hands on her hips and moved her back where she had been.

"Oh, no, I'm not making it that easy," he chuckled. "Besides, I like you rubbing your pussy against my cock right here on the street." He nibbled her neck then returned his lips to her ear. "A bus just went past, and everyone on it saw you getting yourself off. All the pedestrians, all the drivers...they're all looking at you, thinking you're a hot little slut."

"And that we're both drunk, because adults just don't act like this when they're sober."

His voice was pushing her. He still had her hips in his grasp and was moving her, getting her to push and grind in particular ways that must have been good for him, but were also doing crazy things to her. "They'll never know," he said, his voice gravelly with desire, "that you're doing this because I told you to. But you'll know, won't you?"

Each word felt like a lick on her clit. Her body began to tremble uncontrollably, and she pressed her face against his chest, trying not to scream.

"You're going to come for me right now." It wasn't a question.

The trembling turned to violent shakes. Her pussy spasmed, and she wished Jack was inside her. The street around her vanished, lost in a flood of sensation.

And despite herself, Serena did scream, muffled against Jack's broad chest.

He shifted so his arms were around her, possessively but far more gently than they had been, and he cuddled her close, nuzzling at her hair. "Good girl," he said. "That's my good girl." The pride and desire in his voice danced across Serena's skin and caused little aftershocks in her dripping pussy.

And he just held her that way until she stopped trembling, as seemingly oblivious to other people during this tender moment as he had been during the lewd one.

After that, the only real question was whose place they would go to, and that one was simple. Serena had a roommate, Jack didn't. And so they headed to where Jack had left his car.

On a quiet side street in the financial district, Jack stopped her. "Take off your panties," he ordered abruptly.

"Wha...?" Serena hoped she didn't look as foolish as she sounded.

"I bet they're soaked through. Aren't they?"

She nodded mutely. They had been at least since he'd fed her the squid, but articulating that was too much for her brain at the moment.

"Already sticky enough out tonight without sticky panties, too. So lose them."

She looked around. The street was deserted except for a couple of men having a smoke outside the restaurant on the corner. They were apparently having a heated conversation, unlikely to pay attention to something happening up the block. Still, it seemed a little public. Being pantyless wasn't the problem; no one would ever know for sure under her full-skirted sundress unless she tripped or had some other accident so spectacular that lack of underwear would be the least of her worries. It was getting them off gracefully.

She hesitated, half of her screaming to obey Jack and see what further adventures it led to, the other half too embarrassed to move.

"Problem?" he asked, in a tone she couldn't read.

Serena nodded, then shook her head. Why was this so hard? She'd slithered out of wet bikini bottoms under a skirt before; it was the same principle.

"We haven't talked about limits yet, or set any ground rules. You can say no. I'd just want to know why if you do, if it's a hard limit or just something you're not ready for tonight."

And knowing that she could say no somehow made it easier to say yes, and to work the panties down while leaning on him for balance.

By the time she bent down to retrieve them from around her ankle, she could feel her juices on the top of her thighs.

Before she could shove them into her bag, Jack embraced her, gently enough, but effectively pinioning her arms to her sides.

The panties hung limp in her hand—the hand that was facing the street, for anyone to see.

Despite an overwhelming urge to crunch the tiny thong into her fist, she didn't move. Part of her brain that she wouldn't have thought could function under these conditions recognized the test and saw the right, desired—desirable—answer in the same blinding flash.

Jack liked teasing. Jack liked testing. Jack wanted to know what she wanted, what she didn't want, what her limits were; but they hadn't had a chance to talk about it yet. And by letting her know she could say no, he'd forced her to think about whether her urge to curl up and die was merely a knee-jerk reaction.

It was.

All this flashed through her brain in a millisecond. Then he kissed her and all efforts at thinking pretty much stopped.

There was laughter and the sound of footsteps.

She opened her eyes, peered around Jack as best she could.

A small group of older women was approaching, all wearing logo caps from a popular tourist pub and giggling as if they'd spent the early evening sampling the pub's wares. Gray-haired and solid looking, dressed in clothes that owed more to comfort than fashion, they reminded her of her mom.

Panic flared.

And then faded. Funny, but with Jack's arms around her, she felt safe to do things she'd only fantasized about before. Not that she'd especially fantasized about showing a bunch of motherly strangers what a tart she was, but "forced" exhibitionism had definitely been in her top ten masturbatory hits.

"You're thinking too much again," Jack murmured, and resumed the kiss.

As the tipsy tourists passed them, she overheard a shocked—or maybe amused—exclamation of "Now that's not something you see every day!" and a lot more laughter.

Serena trembled and clenched, so excited by the situation and the fact of being caught that she was almost ready to come again without being touched.

"Time to get you home, my girl," Jack whispered in her ear.

And those words, that possessive tone was all it took to bring her off again, coming on the streets of the financial district for the second time that night.

ANIMAL INSIDE

Neve Black

I felt the waves of excitement washing over me as I stood on my tiptoes and reached for the shoebox marked in black felt-tipped pen: *Animal Inside*. I carefully lifted the exotic ocelot, red patent leather, open-toed, four-and-a-half-inch spiked heels with red vinyl piping and sexy ankle straps from the box. I tenderly caressed them, petting the fur before slipping them onto my bare feet. I felt invincible and crazy-sexy whenever I wore these shoes. I felt the animal inside me stir.

It had to be pushing one hundred degrees outside. It was windy, and the air was oppressively thick with humidity. Standing in the foyer, I peeled off my damp, red cotton blouse; khaki skirt; beige cotton panties and bra from my sweat-soaked body. I stood there naked, wearing only my shoes, and let the air conditioner cool me down before walking the few steps into the bathroom. I enjoyed feeling my nipples harden as the chilly air greeted them. I loved the clicking sound my shoes made as they tapped against the crème marble floor underfoot.

The bathroom countertop and large walk-in shower were also opaque, crème marble. A pristine white claw-foot bathtub with shiny, chrome fixtures stood next to the shower. The toilet was located just past the chocolate-stained cabinets that surrounded the sink. The bathroom's walls were covered with soft lavender and off-white paisley print wallpaper. It was beautiful, as always, and I took a deep breath in. I slowly moved my neck from side to side as I let out a long and luxurious sigh. It felt wonderful being there.

There was a hole in the bathroom wall. The hole was at eye level, located between the shower and the toilet, and it was the size of a quarter in diameter and about three inches in depth. You wouldn't have noticed it unless you knew it was there, even though the hole went clear through to the other side of the scant wall.

Wearing only my shoes, I stood in front of the mirror over the bathroom sink. I pulled the elastic hair band from my wavy, golden-brown, shoulder-length hair. I gazed at my reflection: the crow's feet surrounding my round blue eyes seemed less prominent in this light. I moved in closer to the mirror to further analyze my face. The vertical creases around my wide mouth and plump lips weren't as noticeable as they had been this morning, and what I'd thought looked a lot like a bing cherry-sized pimple poking out from the cleft in my chin earlier today had faded into a blushing smudge. Everything seemed to look and feel better in room number 252.

I ran my fingers through my sweaty hair, releasing all the kinks and knots from its being wind-whipped outside in the soaring heat. I ran my hands down the sides of my petite frame, touching the outsides of my small, alert breasts, moving down to my flat stomach and gently combing the threads of my soft pubic hair with my short, unpolished nails.

I heard the sound of someone's voice coming through the wall from the bathroom in the room next door. Perhaps they were speaking into the telephone, or maybe they were having a conversation with someone else. I couldn't tell.

Eagerly, my fingertips reached for the eyebrow tweezers I'd left on the bathroom countertop. I moved toward the hole in the wall. The pads of my fingers located the slightly worn-edged, cut-out circle around the wallpaper in the wall. The cutout was inserted with a long, cylinder-shaped piece of hard foam.

Like a doctor performing surgery, I inserted the tweezers around the foam's outer edges. The foam was nicked and scraped from where the tweezers had greeted it in the past. I pulled the foam out about an inch, until my thumb and index finger could easily grasp onto the tube and pull it all the way out, announcing the hole's presence.

The hole in the wall was much more than just a peephole between the two bathrooms. It was a portal to the animal inside me. The world I lived in didn't allow for creatures unless they were on a leash and restrained. In room 252, animals were given permission to roam freely.

I stepped in closer, closing one eye, while pressing my other eye to the hole, peering into the room next door. I was looking into the familiar, but the unknown at the same time. I felt my pussy getting wet. I felt my clit begin to ping, and the animal inside me stretched and yawned, waking up from a slumber.

I gazed into the hole, and my eye searched the bathroom, a mirror image of the one I was standing in. Because of the hole's size and depth, I couldn't see the bathroom panoramically; I could only see one small and specific area at a time.

At first my eye saw a black, leather toiletry case sitting on the counter. My eye changed focus and moved onto a crumpled heap of clothes that lay on the floor next to the bathtub, and then I saw a shadow being cast toward the bathroom door's entrance.

My eye searched left to right, up and then down, and I couldn't see anyone at first, and then, standing in the bathroom doorway, I saw a man's bare feet, plus his ankles and knees. His feet moved toward me, and I had to adjust my eye again to see.

He stopped, and my eye fixated on his flaccid cock as it poked out from his thick, unruly, burnt-orange pubic hair. He stood still, facing the wall, standing just in front of the shower, and I could hear his breath deepen. He was staring at the hole—at me—but I knew he couldn't see me. I was camouflaged. I was protected behind the wood, drywall, carpenter's nails and paint that obscured me. I knew he knew the animal inside was close by though.

I heard the shower handle being turned as the old pipes squeaked, and the water began sputtering from the showerhead as it was forced upward from the bowels below.

I heard the water as it was running down the shower's walls, and I saw his hand slowly moving up and down along the shaft of his cock. Curiously, he left the shower door open. My eye followed him as he squatted down in front of the opened shower door. He spread his legs and faced me.

As my one eye watched him, the water began to fall more steadily. Its pervasive force spattered and sprayed outside the open shower door and puddled onto the floor around him. The water splashed onto one side of his wide shoulders; his expansive, hairy chest and protruding belly.

"You like to watch," he said, while he rubbed his cock. It wasn't a question, it was a statement.

The water was targeting the back of his right hand, as he moved it faster up and down along his shaft. He'd loosen his kung-fu grip and slide his fingertips over the head, wet from his precome and the deluge of water. He'd move his hand back and forth across his shaft again, squeezing and massaging his now semihardened cock.

"What are you wearing?" he asked. He remained unanswered.

"Are you touching yourself while you watch me stroke my dick?" He fired another question at me.

My clit was beginning to pulsate, and my pussy lips felt gluttonous: full and juicy. I moved my eye upward and away from his cock, until I saw his small, pursed lips; large, hawklike nose and a full head of wavy, burnished hair. His small black eyes were fixed on the hole, on me, and he moaned and grunted while he masturbated, waiting for me to respond to his questions.

The air conditioner was turned way up, but my skin felt hot and feverish. I was light-headed, and I could feel the beads of sweat start to run down the back of my neck, dripping down my spine and settling between the crack of my ass. I stood there watching him, watching his cock get harder and listening as his breath quickened. I slipped my right hand between my legs. I let my fingers slide back and forth across my engorged clit. "*Ooooh, that's the spot; right there,*" I whispered as I watched him start to jitter and grunt while his hand continued to move faster up and down.

"Wh—" He started to ask another question.

"Yes. God. Yes. I love watching, and watching you makes me incredibly wet. I have to touch myself. I'm touching my slippery, wet pussy. It's swollen and pulsating." The animal inside me finally spoke, cutting him off, and the words penetrated through the wall to him.

"Ooooh, god," he said, moaning.

I pushed my fingers deep inside my pussy, then pulled them out, only to push them frantically inside again, applying circular pressure up against my G-spot. My eye was still watching him, while my fingers pleasured myself, and I could feel my knees begin to weaken.

"What are you wearing?" he asked for the second time, as he stroked his cock faster.

"I'm completely naked...except for my sexy, animal-print shoes with four-and-a-half-inch red patent leather heels," I finally answered, speaking into the wall slowly. My voice was low and guttural, induced by the animal shoes that evoked the animal inside me.

He tilted his head back and opened his mouth and asked in a baritone, raspy growl, "Are they...are they...closed...or open...toed?"

"Open...you can see my painted, bright-red toenails peeking through," I answered.

He moaned loudly. His cock was very hard now, and I could tell he was getting close to coming. I was so turned on watching and listening as he reached the edge of release. My pussy was dripping and engorged, and I kept pushing my two fingers in and out while I made circular movements against my clit with the palm of my hand.

"Oh, I want to fuck you hard. I want to hear those open-toed shoes scrape across the floor as I spread your legs, bend you over and fuck you hard with my dick." His voice was loud, and he was breathing hard and panting as he neared orgasm. His eyes were closed, and the water spattered onto his face, mixed with the beads of sweat that lined his brow.

I imagined his hard cock had replaced my fingers, fucking me in and out and in and out. "Yes. God, yes, I want you to fuck me hard with your cock." Both my voice and the animal's voice roared into the wall, speaking over the sledgehammer pounding in my chest, the shower streaming down, and the sound of his hand *thwack, thwack, thwacking* away on his cock.

My clit was thrumming against my hand now; I was going to come.

"I'm going to come. I'm going to come all over your cock." I said loudly, and I threw my head back, taking my eye away from the hole as my body was wracked by the spasms of orgasm.

"Ooooh. I'm coming, I'm coming, I'm coming all over your open-toed animal pumps...and your red-painted toes...and..." he yelled out to me as I heard him grunt and moan.

I stood there for a moment, catching my breath before I pushed the foam back into the wall and covered up the hole. I slipped into the shower and washed the sweat and slick juices that had spilled from between my legs. As I turned the shower off, I could hear my cell phone ringing from inside my handbag in the next room. I wondered if it was my husband calling to find out what was for dinner, or maybe it was the babysitter calling about one of the kids. My day-to-day world started to seep back into my stolen pleasurable moment.

I toweled off and slipped back into the same clothes I'd left in the foyer earlier. As I made my way into the lobby to check out, I could see a man talking on his cell phone as he leaned up against one of the lobby's pillars. He was dressed in a brown suit, and as I rounded the corner, I could see his reddish hair. It was him, my animal's liaison from that afternoon. I glanced over at him, but he wasn't paying any attention; he didn't even notice my shoes because he, too, was being pulled back into his daily life.

I placed the room key on the front desk, and the clerk smiled and asked me, "Was everything okay, Mrs. Smith?"

"Yes. It was wonderful. Thank you." I said smiling.

"Great. Would you like to go ahead and book room 252 for next month, then?" the clerk asked me.

"Yes, please," I said, still smiling, lifting my handbag over my shoulder and moving across the marble hotel floor, shoes clicking as I made my way outside and back to my nonanimal life that awaited me just past the hotel's front door.

THE LONDON O

Justine Elyot

It had swiftly become a matter of pride to Lloyd that he should provide more, bigger, better orgasms than any of my previous lovers and, in the early days of our relationship, I confess that I might have played on this tiny insecurity.

"Orlando was so well named," I teased over moules marinières in some Café Rouge or another. "An O at either end." I ran the point of my tongue over the tender morsel in its creamy broth-filled shell. "He had the gift."

"Either end?" Lloyd's light tone did nothing to fool me. He knew a challenge when he heard one. "You mean he gave you an orgasm in your toes? And the top of your head?"

"The location isn't important," I grinned, swirling the lascivious mollusk around the insides of my mouth before swallowing.

"Au contraire, Miss Martin, the location is a critical factor. Don't you agree?"

Lloyd sipped sagely at his red wine, his eyes narrowed, keen to pursue the conversational line.

"Well, without wanting to get too graphic at the dinner table…"

"Oh, no, I'm not talking body geography. I know the map of Sophie well enough, and I don't care how well-thumbed it is. I know where to plant my flag when I want her earth to move. I'm talking about places."

"Places? Orgasmic places?"

"Yeah. Where's the strangest place you ever climaxed?"

"Oh…well. A swimming pool. An underground parking lot. A hotel balcony." I frowned in an effort of memory.

"Tame stuff. Vanilla in the extreme. I'm surprised at you."

"Lloyd! Where am I supposed to do it? Onstage?"

"That would add spice." His louche grin was as wide as a wolf's, and his knee nudged mine beneath the checkered cloth. "I'm sure you'd find an appreciative audience."

"So where's your most outrageous spot for hitting the spot, then? Since you see yourself as the voice of experience here."

"There was a croquet lawn. A rowing boat. An aircraft hangar. And that was all before I left college."

"So what is the point you are making? Were those orgasms better?"

"No, they weren't better," he conceded. "But they had a quality all of their own. Didn't you find that with your experiences outside the bedroom?"

"I suppose I did. Yes."

"But nobody has ever pursued that with you?"

"No. I must admit, my past lovers have mainly wanted privacy. Don't you?"

"There's a time and a place."

I snorted.

"That appears to be the *opposite* of what you're proposing.

You seem to be saying that any time and any place are fine for sex."

"Not sex necessarily. Just having an orgasm. Coming. Oh, I love that. Coming. Such an innocent word; such a coy little euphemism."

"Okay, now I'm struggling."

"You will be. Finish that up. I'm getting the bill. I need to show you what I mean and in this case, I think actions will speak louder than words."

I mopped up the last of the delicious sauce with a hunk of baguette and pushed the plate aside.

"Just coming," I said.

Outside it had begun to rain; Lloyd grasped my hand and held on to me, weaving me through the shining streets, between phalanxes of umbrellas, down to Soho, where the pavement narrowed and we had to maintain strict single file until we reached the forlorn last bastion of that district's seedy past. On Brewer Street, the red and blue neon flickered from the doorways; the rain conferred a strange and poignant glamour to the scene. Lloyd and I were frequent visitors to this historic fleshpot; I'm sure some of the patrons of the row of sex boutiques must have wondered if we had furnished our entire flat from their stock. I used to order that kind of thing online, but Lloyd converted me to the "experience" and the "ambience" and, most importantly, the exquisite, needling shame of handing my purchases over the counter. I both hated and loved it, but now I had the taste for it.

Through a rainbow-colored door curtain we passed, its plastic strips sliding coldly across our wet faces, into a brightly lit outpost of Sodom and Gomorrah.

"Evenin'," we were greeted laconically by the vast biker who presided over this empire of extravagant sin. Lloyd tipped his head and the man returned to his *Standard* without further interrogation.

"What are we looking for?" I asked Lloyd in a whisper as he led me beyond the lurid DVD covers and gnarly latex phalluses, even past the spanking and bondage section where we had spent many happy browsing hours.

"Knickers," he murmured, heading through an archway to a small square room populated by headless mannequins in PVC basques. Then he looked at me with a salacious smirk. "Whore's drawers."

"What's underwear got to do with it?" I wondered, having well and truly lost the connection between al fresco climax and these scanty scraps of hideous nylon.

"Hmm," was the only reply I got, Lloyd being now completely absorbed in the racks and shelves of cheap tartwear.

"Crotchless?" I hazarded, fingering a plastic peephole bra and slit panty set.

"Quite the opposite. No, not that...where the hell are they? I *saw* them here, I'm sure I did...aha!"

He wheeled around in triumph, brandishing a clear plastic bag containing what looked like an ordinary pair of black lacy briefs. But that was not all it contained. A remote control unit sat alongside the garment...remote-controlled knickers? *Oh!*

"I think I've heard of these," I said guardedly, stretching out a hand for further inspection. He handed over the bag, confirming my suspicions. Attached to the gusset at strategic intervals were a clitoral stimulator and a vibrator. "Are you serious?"

"Are you scared?" he taunted, taking the bag back and rustling it in my face, making ghostly *woo woo* noises. "Attack of the knickers!"

"They're expensive," I noted.

"I think they'd be worth it," he said, his voice a broken

croon. He had that glazed look in his eyes that he always gets when he's imagining devilish and deviant practices. "Oh, the fun I could have with you…in these."

"So that's what you mean when you talk about odd locations for orgasms. In theory, I could have one anywhere at all…if I was wearing these."

"Yes. Anywhere at all. If I pressed the button…oh, the power! It could go to my head."

"I think it's already gone to somewhere else," I remarked, glancing down at his bulging trouser crotch.

As ever, it was my task to hand the purchase over the counter while Lloyd did the credit card bit. As ever, I crimsoned, prayed that no comment would be passed, no eye contact made. Eye contact, of a knowing kind, *was* made, but the comment was reserved for Lloyd.

"No returns, I'm afraid," he said. "Same as with all the other vibes. I'm sure you'll be satisfied with it though."

I was staring stonily at some massage oils, refusing to look up at their no doubt expansive grins and winks.

"Have you road tested one yourself?" Lloyd asked. *Oh, come on, let's go.*

"Yeah. I'd recommend it. Very quiet, no annoying buzzing. So you can wear them…anywhere."

"Thanks. I'll bear that in mind."

The shopkeeper was right. The vibrator unit was indeed almost inaudible, as I discovered on the tube journey home, having been persuaded to change my knickers in a pavement toilet cubicle before descending the escalator. Riding smoothly down on the moving staircase, past drinkers and diners and late-working office types, I was highly conscious of the difference. The fabric was snug and tight, so that the vibrator attachment was firmly lodged inside and the cold rippled latex of the clitoral stimulator nudged and rubbed exactly as advertised.

"How does it feel?" whispered Lloyd, standing beside me, one hand placed possessively on my bum, rubbing my skirt as if this would wear through and reveal the answer.

"Very, very rude," I replied. "Wicked and indecent. I really hope I don't have some kind of accident on the way home. I do not want to end up in Casualty wearing these."

"Does it fill you? Are you wet? Does it rub against your clit?"

"Yes to all three. Shut up, for god's sake!"

"Oh, no, I want you to know you're wearing it; I don't want you to be able to forget. And I want you to know that I know. God, this is turning me on. I hope there aren't any delays on the Northern Line tonight."

We stepped off the escalator and I made a concerted effort to try and walk normally, notwithstanding the exquisite pressure on my clit and the large fake cock wedged in my pussy.

"It's giving you a sensational wiggle," said Lloyd admiringly, falling behind me to survey my swaying backside. "It looks so *obvious* that your pussy is stuffed. But I suppose I know it is, which makes a difference. Maybe nobody else would guess."

I was convinced that everybody knew it as we headed on to the platform. Every passerby, from the teenage youths clicking teeth and sucking back high-energy sodas to the elderly, suited man reading his *Telegraph*, was perfectly cognizant of the fact that I was wearing vibrating knickers, the crotch soaked, my pussy wrapped around a plastic cock, because I was a dirty slut who loves to come and can't get enough orgasms.

Lloyd kept putting his hand into his jacket pocket, teasing me with the fear that he might be about to activate the vibrator, causing me to clamp my thighs together and clench my pelvic-floor muscles. By the time the train came roaring through the tunnel, though, he had still not pressed the magic button.

The train was about three-quarters full, and we could not find a seat together, so I sat in the center of one row while he took a place by the door, at the end of the opposite bank. Sitting like that, with a highly-perfumed lady on one side and a gay punk on the other, I was suddenly sure that people might be able to see up my skirt somehow, even though it was knee length and didn't even give away the fact that I was wearing stockings ordinarily. I decided to cross my legs, but this pushed the nubbed rubber even farther into my swimming clit and made my pussy feel even fuller, an inescapable sensation. I squirmed against the seat cushion, unsure whether to uncross my legs again, and Lloyd chose that moment to flip my switch.

I had to swallow a cry as the invasive presence in my pussy began to rev up, a slow shudder at first, speeding to an almost unbearable throb. It felt so painfully wanton that I knew my climax would not be put off for long. I sat back, stretching my spine, trying my very hardest not to pant or moan. My pussy lips twitched and my nipples were hard and sore, pushing against the lace of my bra until some of the pattern must have transferred to them. Lloyd's sly, delighted smile accentuated the hot rush of sensation; he had had to put a copy of the *Evening Standard* over his crotch to hide the excitement of it all. My nether regions seemed to be flexing and rippling beyond any vestige of muscular control; the vibrator whizzed up to maximum speed, my clit was swollen and struggling to barge past the little rubber stimulators, my cheeks were hotter than fire and I was fidgeting so much that my neighbors forewent the customary Tube etiquette of complete-oblivion-to-all and began looking sideways at me. And then I came, pressing my hands down into my lap, trying to breathe through the intense flood of liquid sweetness, shuffling my bottom against the cushion and biting down on my lip.

And we were still only at Goodge Street. It had taken less than five minutes to make me come in public on the dusty upholstery of Transport for London.

The gay punk and the perfumed lady moved to the left and right respectively, making no secret of their desire to distance themselves. I couldn't blame them. I was sure the heavy odor of my arousal and satisfaction must have been hanging in the air, breaking the barrier of the woman's civet-drenched fragrance and the gay punk's patchouli. I spent the rest of the journey looking daggers at Lloyd, or as many daggers as I could muster in the face of the great awe and wonder his sheer perversion engendered in my spirit.

By the time we arrived at Highgate, it was clear that we would never make the journey from the station to our flat without Lloyd's cock punching a hole through his trousers. We ran with our respective hindrances of an erection and a pair of vibrating knickers as quickly as we could up the path and into the wooded area that stood so conveniently at the side of the Archway Road where the underground came overground. Lloyd shoved me unceremoniously against the bark of a tree, my breasts pushing against the rough wood, and hitched my skirt to the waist, pulling down the back of the knickers to expose my bottom to the fresh night air. Yards away from us, rail passengers mooched up and down the pathway, and the late night traffic rumbled and lumbered. The nearby street provided just enough low yellow light to give us a few visual clues as to how to go about our swift and urgent coupling. Lloyd did not quite pull the panties down, leaving the vibrator where it lay.

"I want your arse," he muttered, priming it with a thumb that he had bathed in the juices of my overworked clit. "You can keep that thing on. I'm going to switch it on now." Once more, to my consternated delight, the stiff obstruction in my pussy began to buzz and throb, though the clit stimulator was only half in place now, giving way to the more pressing issue of Lloyd's easy access. Once I was relaxed enough to take two of Lloyd's fingers in my tiny, tight hole, he decided he could hold back no longer, unzipping hurriedly and pushing his damp cockhead between my spread cheeks.

The vibe swelled and filled me as he eased the bulbous tip through my rear pucker. We moaned in concert; I from delirious fullness, he from long-anticipated relief. The farther in he slid, the wider and fatter and more apt to split I felt inside, until I had no sensation anywhere other than that seat of basest needs. I was a pussy and arsehole, full and well used, as I should be.

"Look at you," grunted Lloyd, once he was fully sheathed, his balls gently dangling against my lower cheeks. "Getting your arse fucked against a tree, with a full pussy. I bet Orlando never did that for you."

"N-no," I admitted, though my voice came out as a trickle of a quiver. "Oh. No."

"So who's the orgasm-meister now, eh?" He began to pull his shaft back, slowly, switching every nerve ending to its brightest setting on the way. "Who makes you come the hardest?"

"You do," I assured him, pushing my bum back, inviting him back in with all the urgency I could muster.

He was halfway along now, and I could not bear it if he pulled all the way out. I tried to clamp my muscles down on him, but it was difficult, and it stung.

"Who has the hottest, kinkiest plans for you, Sophie? Who knows exactly what kind of a dirty, nasty girl you are?"

"Oh, you, oh, you." He slammed back in and I hissed blissfully.

"Yes, me. Nobody else. Not fucking *Orlando*. Me. I'm the man for you."

He began to thrust hard, forcing my pelvis into the desiccated bark, the tip of his cock nudging against the rounded end of the vibrator with each uncompromising plunge into my rudest depths. I imagined the two cocks, real and simulated, joining together and making one long, pitiless invader, keeping that back-and-forth rhythm going from pussy to arsehole and back, forever and without end. The tree trunks here were narrow enough to wrap my arms around, and I clung on for dear life, hanging there while Lloyd gripped my hips and dug deeper and harder than I had thought possible. I knew I would be sore along there for a day or so, but I knew also that each shift and squirm in my office chair would make me smile and glow with the memory. The combination of the vibrator and the cock sent me into a roaring chaos of orgasm that I nevertheless had to keep quiet about, just as on the tube, for fear of disturbing the public. Lloyd froze behind me, then sent a long, sibilant hiss out through the trees before soaking my arse with his plentiful seed, sending jet after jet up, one after the other.

"God, you could have been made for me," he panted, his head on my shoulder for an exhausted moment, before straightening up and making himself decent once again. I could not quite make myself decent, still in the vibe knickers, which were becoming itchy and too wet to wear without an obvious slicking sound when I walked, not to mention a large stain spreading across my backside and sticking the material to my skin, but I somehow made it back to our flat, feeling that every passerby knew my secret and was giving Lloyd a knowing wink behind my back.

Still, we thought the new addition to our toy box a very valuable one, and the vibrating panties have had innumerable outings since their memorable debut. I wore them in the British Museum, on the London Eye, at the cinema in Leicester Square and picnicking in Hyde Park. They were always just the thing to brighten up a dull day, and we came very close to fulfilling Lloyd's ambition of making me come, hard and long, in every tourist attraction in the City. Most unforgettably, I began to sweat and puff in the middle of Buckingham Palace and had to sit on a velvet chair pulled out for me by one of the security guards.

"She's having one of her turns," said Lloyd laconically, winking at the man, before taking me out and having me down on the Victoria Embankment.

So when it comes down to the question of who provides more, bigger, better orgasms, Lloyd is the hands-down winner. He is also the hands-free winner. I really don't think Orlando will ever be able to catch up now.

FIGHT

Charlotte Stein

She knows what he's got her for her birthday. He always gets her the best presents, but this year is extraspecial. This year, she knows—it's going to be a fight.

In the morning, he acts real casual. Like maybe it's going to be nothing. Perhaps he's going to give her some flowers or some chocolates or some perfume, frivolous things that past boyfriends always got her, because she's a girl and girls like that. Right?

But Gray knows she doesn't like that. He knows she likes spiky and sassy and what's about to come to her any minute now. She can feel the anticipation prickling over the nape of her neck; over her belly, like a rough hand passing there; between her legs, where things are already getting sticky and heated.

Any minute now, she thinks and bites her lip instead of the sandwich in front of her.

Gray, however, continues to eat his bacon on wholemeal as though nothing's going to happen. He chews, studiously. This bacon sandwich is the most important thing in the entire world. Why, they could create university courses on the art of bacon sandwich eating!

Just look at me, Elle, eating my delicious breakfast. The rhythmic motion of my jaw. Swallowing slow. Tongue coming out to flicker over my sauce-streaked lip—

She stops pretending to be interested in her own sandwich. His is far more compelling, and it gets even more so when he sucks grease from his long, thick fingers. His lips work all the way to the webbing between and then execute a slow, easy, lewd slide back up again. And then down again. And then it's just his eager pink tongue curling around the tip of his finger while his eyes look down on her.

She thinks of all the porn she's ever watched. That's what he looks like, licking bacon off his fingers: like all the porn she's ever watched.

Even worse, he seems intrigued by his own wet finger and with eyes intent on her, he leans back in the creaky old kitchen chair and unbuttons his shirt with his other hand; slides that wet finger into the unseen space beneath the material, to rub that wetness someplace nice.

Her own nipples ache in sympathy. He arches his back; the shape of his hand beneath the wing of his shirt circles, circles. When his lips part, she wants to part hers, too.

The fight is on, it seems, and he is already winning. He's almost made her come just by touching himself.

But then he knows how much that turns her on. It's what's going to tip the scales in his favor, through this little who-can-give-the-other-the-most-and-biggest-orgasms fight. He knows so, so much about her—and sometimes has that knowledge without even asking, as though he has a preternatural sex sense, always sniffing out her kinks and desires.

Whereas she…well, sometimes it's obvious what he wants or likes. His nipples are very sensitive. He enjoys talking dirty and having someone talk dirty to him. He likes teasing and being teased.

But sometimes it's not so obvious. Sometimes she has to figure him out, like a Rubik's Cube made out of man-flesh. Just like now, when it *seems* as though he's doing this just to push her to the edge, but it could also be that he loves disarming her as much as she loves being disarmed.

As she watches, he unbuttons the remainder of his shirt, spreads it open so that she can see the lean stripe of his torso, the coarse mess of his chest hair. In many ways, his features are quite feminine—that plump lower lip, his big soft eyes—but his body isn't. It's rough and hairy and sinewy with muscle, broad shouldered and big dicked.

Still, he plays with it the way she imagines girls do: slyly and sensuously, putting on a show for some burly boyfriend. He teases his sharp nipples and his shivering belly, always with his eyes on her. And then the show progresses to him pushing one hand down his pants.

There's something about that sight—of a man with his hand inside his jeans, as though he has to be furtive and dirty—that sings straight to her clit. She can feel it swelling and stiffening, her entire sex plumping until it's all pressed nice and hard against the material of her knickers. If she rocks on her chair, slippery flesh eases against slippery flesh.

But she doesn't rock, beyond that first little tryout. If she goes for it again, she knows she'll come, just like that—like a kid creaming in his shorts.

When his hand stirs rhythmically beneath the line of his jeans and his eyes flutter briefly shut and he groans gutturally, she has to squeeze her nails into her thighs.

"Am I making you wet?" he asks, but then he cocks his head and reconsiders. "Why am I asking? Of course I am. Your cheeks are flushed and I can see your nipples through that T-shirt. Does the material feel good, rubbing against them?"

She forces herself not to reply. None of his questions are really questions, anyway.

"My hand feels good on my cock. I'm so hard. Jesus. I bet this would feel good, buried in your cunt. I think I'll jerk off though, first—take the edge off."

"That'll count," she blurts out, but those aren't the words she wants to say. She wants to tell him, *Oh, yes, please, god, fuck me, fuck me, fuck my cunt,* but instead blusters on with this: "That will count as one for me. If you jerk off and come while looking at me like that, it counts as one goal for me."

He raises one eyebrow.

"So you're going to play dirty, huh?"

"Those are the rules."

"But I really, really want to mess up the insides of my jeans," he whines— though it's not a real whine. His mouth curls up at the corners, just a little.

"Then do it. Go on and do it, you dirty fucker. I bet you've done it loads of times before—at university, maybe? Sitting in the lecture hall, bored shitless by Professor Snoozefest's presentation on the life cycle of bees. Maybe some big-titted undergrad was sitting below you, and you could see right down her top—"

"That doesn't sound like me..."

"—So you just pressed the heel of your palm against your straining-against-your-fly dick, and rubbed and rubbed until you blew your wad into your jeans."

"...I guess it could be me, if you like that idea."

His hand has sped up beneath the material. She can see it.

She can see the flush high up on his cheeks, too, the slight rock to his hips.

"I bet you got all sweaty and red faced, just like you are now. I bet when you came, you made a noise you had to stifle with your hand."

He closes his eyes, leans his head briefly back. His hips bump right up at nothing, and she's sure she can see his hand squeezing hard at the base of his dick.

"Like the one I'm going to be making soon?" he asks.

"Not if you keep pinching off your orgasm like you're doing now, cheater."

"Ah—it's not cheating. It's only making me come faster—shit!"

"Do it harder, then. Really squeeze."

"Like you sometimes do?"

"Yeah, like that. Get a handful of your balls and tug down hard."

"Oh, oh, man...you know doing all of that nonsense only gets me off quicker."

"And talking about it?"

"And talking about it gets me off quicker—you're the fucking cheat."

"Just stop touching yourself, then."

He moans, loud and long. Gasps, suddenly breathless.

"I can't. Fuck, I can't—ah, you bitch."

His entire body stiffens and twists, mouth open, eyes scrunched shut. His hips buck and jerk as though there's something more than his hand just above him, and then she can hear the extra slickness. Can hear him stroking through his own spunk, as he ekes out the remainder of his orgasm.

She's as surprised as he is to find she knows him much better than either of them thought.

It doesn't take him long to even the score. He cleans himself up with his tongue—long wet swipes over come-slicked fingers—until she is forced to masturbate at the sight. It only takes a couple of taps against her well-oiled clit to make her call out his name, but unfortunately for her, that only lays the table.

Now she wants the meal. Apparently, so does he.

"Was that good?" he asks, soft and drawling. His eyes are heavy-lidded, a sensuous look that would usually indicate satisfaction—but not now. She can practically smell his hunger for more, and it seems he's able to do the same in kind.

"Not quite good enough, huh? Well, bend over the table and maybe I'll see to that for you."

She shakes her head, but her mouth won't make the actual words.

"No? Come on, bend over the table and lift your skirt. Lift it up nice and high so I can see that juicy slit. Maybe you can even grab hold of your asscheeks and spread them wide for me. What do you say?"

She says nothing. Her closed eyes say it all for her, as does the way she swallows and shivers.

"You've spread for guys before, right? Those two guys you once shared a flat with that you told me about? You must have spread for both of them at some point. They came home drunk, caught you watching nasty porn. One in your mouth, one in your pussy...or maybe not your mouth. One in your ass, right?"

She doesn't shake her head for him this time, though in this instance, it's definitely untrue. So good, but untrue—like all the dirty tales they tell each other.

"Did they fuck you at the same time? One in each hole—what a nasty whore you are. I'm going to have to come in your mouth and your pussy and your ass just to make up for all that dirty business. Don't you think?"

In answer, she stands on shaky legs and bends over the kitchen table. But he doesn't laugh or crow in triumph. She just hears his chair being knocked over and his clothes being shucked in a tearing rush, and then he's behind her. Oh, god, he's behind her, on his knees.

She can't hate him for the point he wins with his tongue swirling and sliding through her slit. Her entire body sobs when she comes—hard enough to cream all over his face and make dents in the edges of the table where she's gripping.

But she can hate him for winning a third point, when he stands too suddenly and sinks his thick cock all the way in. Just a few short, well-aimed thrusts, and she stutters into orgasm again.

However, the haze of pleasure doesn't rob her of reason or the aim of the game. She waits for him to settle, to ease into a false sense of security—still lodged in her pussy but unaware of the danger.

And then she forces herself back, until he's trapped between her body and the kitchen counter.

Of course he tries to squirm away. But it's difficult when your girlfriend has her legs on either side of yours and her pussy's squeezing tight around your cock. She knows it is, because he grunts and groans and tells her *No fair*.

"Stay there and take it," she says, which only makes him worse. He doesn't even try to push on her hips and get her away from him—he just waits and cries out in pleasure when she thrusts back onto him over and over.

She feels him clutch a handful of her skirt together at the small of her back. After a moment, he uses it to yank her onto his cock.

"You like that, huh?" she asks, but he can't speak any more than she could earlier. "You like that, you dirty little bitch?"

She hears him sigh in response, sweet and wavering.

"Are you going to come? I bet you are. Come on, give it up."

It's on those words that he obeys.

He thinks he's got her beat, she knows. She's on the ropes. Three to two, and although he's very good at getting hard again, at going for it more than once, more than twice, sometimes more than five times, it's far easier for him to be reluctant.

She curses herself for not figuring on his physical advantage.

And then redoubles her efforts. There's nothing Gray likes more, after all, than a sleepy blow job. It's the perfect trap, too, because as he drifts off in the middle of a sea of satiated kisses and limbs wrapped around him, she knows he thinks he's won.

And when she stirs him from his doze with sweet licks and sucks all the way around his soft but rapidly hardening cock, he's too warm and comfortable and sleepy to resist. His hands tangle in her hair before he's even aware of the time and place.

It's only when he's fully hard and thrusting that he groans in despair and frustration. She can hear it clearly in the sound: I thought I had it. Victory was mine.

Now he just thrusts up at her teasing mouth, hands alternately fisting in the bedsheets and in her hair. He doesn't force her, however—no, no. Forcing is for winners. People on the verge of drawing don't get to call the shots.

Instead, she pins his hips and licks with just the tip of her tongue, until he's writhing and cursing her as hard as she cursed herself, not a moment before. But she waits until he's swollen and straining, until his body trembles like a live wire, and he just has to choke out the words:

"Okay—you win. You win."

It's a lie, but that's not the point. It's not the point at all when she finally swallows him down and feels him arch up into a fierce but near-dry orgasm.

Fighting is about concession, after all—not about keeping score.

SWITCH

Jade Melisande

We are standing at the glass display case at Details, our local piercing studio, peering inside at the body jewelry encased within.

"You sure you want to do this?" my partner, Dylan, asks again. I nod absently. I know he's just being solicitous, but I don't want to be talked out of it. I've made up my mind.

I point to a twelve-gauge ring with a titanium capture bead. "That one," I tell Joe, the piercer. He did the original piercing the first time, but of course he doesn't remember me. That was at least four years ago. "It was a fourteen gauge the first time," I say. "It shouldn't be a problem to go up a size, should it?"

"I don't think so," he says. "We'll take a look."

When I am in the room and lying on the bench seat with my legs spread, Joe pokes around a bit, lifting and looking at the old piercing site in my clitoral hood. It is an entirely clinical setting, and Joe is a consummate professional, and yet I find myself curiously aroused with him peering so closely at me. A strange fantasy floats into my mind, in which my partner, who is sitting across the room, suddenly jumps up and grabs my arms, holding me down so that Joe can use those precise, professional fingers of his—

"How long has it been out?" Joe asks, breaking into my fantasy just when it was getting good.

"Oh, um...three years?" I direct the question at Dylan, as though he would know better than I when it was that I decided to remove my first hood ring. I'd done it the day my divorce went through, as a kind of "fuck you" to my old life, and to the man for whom I had originally gotten it pierced.

Joe nods. "Well, it's not closed up," he says. "I don't have to re-pierce, just reinstall the new ring." At my surprised exclamation, he shrugs. "It's unusual, certainly, but not unheard of." And then he tells me to take a deep breath and pushes the new ring through the old, tight hole.

I swear it hurts worse than the original piercing. I consciously relax my breathing and let the pain wash over me. After a moment, it subsides to a dull pinch. "That's it," says Joe.

I nod, silenced by a sweet rush of heat that floods me. I look up and catch Joe's eyes on me. He grins. "All pierced and ready to play," he says.

"Healing time?" I ask, unconsciously squirming on the bench.

His grin broadens. "It's ready when you are."

I get up cautiously, but there is only a small bit of discomfort—that and a heightened awareness of that sensitive place between my legs. Walking causes my jeans to rub against it, though, and pleasure suffuses me as I do.

By the time Dylan and I get home, my panties are soaked through. I have felt every bump in the road, every slip of the steel against my clitoris, every time my jeans have pressed against the titanium capture bead. As soon as the door is closed behind

Dylan, I spin around and throw myself against him, grinding my cunt against his thigh. The pinch of the ring against my clit is painful and exquisite in its precision.

"Fuck me," I say against his mouth.

He puts his hands on my shoulders and pushes me back a pace. "Should we do that right after you got your ring put back in, Cass?"

I twist out of his hands impatiently, press myself against him again.

"Yes, goddamn it," I say, my voice a snarl of frustration. I haven't been this aroused in I don't know how long. "I want to see if it still works." I knead myself against him, a guttural moaning escaping me as I do.

"You hot little bitch," he says, grabbing a handful of my hair and pulling my head back so he can look into my eyes.

A wide grin splits my face. Oh, yeah, I'm a hot little bitch. "Fuck me," I say again.

He grabs one wrist and spins me around so that my arm is pinned behind my back, then gives me a shove toward the hallway and our bedroom, his hand holding my arm pinned tight the whole way. He pushes me down on the bed as soon as we enter the room, pushing me over so that I am faceup with my arm pinned beneath me. He shoves his knee into my cunt and makes me gasp. I stare up at him, breathing heavily.

"I want to taste the ring in you," he says.

"Yes," I breathe, thrusting my hips upward against his knee. This is why I got the ring put back in.

I had never had an orgasm orally before I got my hood pierced the first time. I hadn't stopped having them after I'd removed it—apparently once the body learns the trick it doesn't forget it—but my orgasms just weren't as powerful, or as easy to achieve.

He unbuttons my jeans and pulls them down without another word. Before he removes my underwear, though, he leans down and buries his face between my legs, his mouth gentle, barely touching the whisper of cloth there. He covers the whole of my mound and lips with his mouth and just breathes on me for a moment. His breath is warm and moist against my cunt, soothing the ache of the piercing, which has begun to throb just a bit. When I start to squirm, he squeezes my thighs where his large hands hold them open and says, without lifting his head, "Be still, Cassie."

I grow still obediently, closing my eyes and leaning my head back. The feel of his mouth sliding over the slippery material is so sensuous, so achingly delicious. I shudder and catch my breath, feeling the sensation building before he's even really started.

He pulls down my underwear then, and I thrust myself up toward his mouth. "Please," I say, wanting to feel his lips on me, his tongue lapping against me, because this is what I have been thinking of, dreaming about, since I decided to put the ring back in.

His first touch is tentative, careful, but my body jerks in shock anyway, the pain/pleasure is so intense.

He stops and looks up at me. "Are you sure this is okay?"

"Yes," I pant. "Yes, please…just…long, flat strokes," I say. "Remember? Like before."

I do not usually instruct him on what I like—he's very good at paying attention to my body's signals—but something has taken me over and I need to have him do it and do it now, just the way I want him to.

And he does. He strokes a flat, wet, warm tongue from my swollen pussy lips all the way up to my tender, throbbing clit. Over and over, long, slow strokes until I am panting and wriggling against his mouth. Intermittently, he takes my clit, hood ring and all, into his mouth and sucks at it gently.

I am riding the waves of pleasure, giving myself over to them, floating and drifting, feeling the ring slide against my clit and his tongue playing with it, building, building toward an orgasm. His fingers tighten on my thighs as he recognizes my excitement building.

"Yes," I say, "yes, yes..."

And then something happens, something in my head. Suddenly he is not fucking me with his mouth—*I* am fucking him with my clit. I begin to thrust my clit against his mouth, *into* his mouth, down his throat, fucking his mouth with a long, extended cocklike clit. I moan and arch against him, shoving my cock-clit into his mouth, growling, twisting my arms out from under me so that I can grab the back of his head, all the better to fuck him.

Is this what he feels as he holds the back of my head, pushing his cock into my mouth over and over? This mindless reaching, thrusting, wanting only to come, to fill his mouth with my come, to feel him gag, to make him swallow every drop?

It is that image that tips me over. I start to orgasm, wave after wave crashing over me. But I'm not coming like a woman, I am coming like a man, thrusting and squirting girl-come into his mouth, filling it, just as he fills mine when he comes in my mouth. Is this what it is like for him, this deep ache and pull, the shuddering release as he spills himself into me? I come clutching my thighs around him, arching my back, holding him pinned to me, and I wonder if this is what it feels like for him, pinning me down with his body, impaling me, as I am impaling him. I come so hard I have to stuff my arm in my mouth to keep from screaming out loud and waking the upstairs neighbors. I come until Dylan finally has to pull himself from my grasp, laughing, gasping for air. I think about the times I have pulled myself away from him gasping for breath that same way, licking the last drops of semen from my lips.

I lean over and pull his face up to mine, lick the salty sweet taste of me from his mouth. I wonder if he felt the force and heat of it squirting down his throat, as I have felt his.

He chuckles at the self-satisfied grin on my face. "I guess it still works, huh?" he says.

Oh, yeah, I think. *It definitely still works.*

ABOUT THE AUTHORS

JACQUELINE APPLEBEE (writing-in-shadows.co.uk) breaks down barriers with smut. Jacqueline's stories have appeared in various anthologies and websites, including Clean Sheets, *Best Women's Erotica, Best Lesbian Erotica, Where the Girls Are* and *Girl Crazy*.

NEVE BLACK has been writing since she can remember and opted for a degree in English Literature. Between studying the classics, Neve discovered she also had affection for writing erotic literature. To learn more about her work, visit neveblack.com.

ANGELA CAPERTON's eclectic erotica spans many genres, including romance, horror, fantasy and what she calls contemporary-with-a-twist. Look for her stories published with Cleis, Circlet Press, Drollerie Press, eXtasy Books and in the indie magazine *Out of the Gutter*. Visit Angela at blog.angelacaperton.com.

HEIDI CHAMPA's work appears in numerous anthologies including *Best Women's Erotica 2010, Frenzy* and *Playing with Fire*. She has also steamed up the pages of *Bust* magazine. If you prefer your erotica in electronic form, she can be found at Clean Sheets, Ravenous Romance, Oysters and Chocolate, and the Erotic Woman. Find her online at heidichampa.blogspot.com.

ELIZABETH COLDWELL's stories have appeared in a variety of anthologies including *Yes, Sir; Bottoms Up; Do Not Disturb* and *The Mile High Club*.

ANDREA DALE's stories have appeared in *Lesbian Cowboys, The Sweetest Kiss* and *Bottoms Up*, among many others. With coauthors, she has sold two novels to Virgin Books. She suspects her smart mouth will either be her undoing or her saving grace. Her website is at cyvarwydd.com.

The joys of erotic writing have been experienced by **ROWAN ELIZABETH** for over five years. Published in *The Best of Best American Erotica 2008, Best Lesbian Love Stories 2009, Hustler* and Ruthie's Club, Rowan has shared her perversions with many like-minded souls (and a few nasty critics). To experience some of Rowan's stories, visit rowanelizabeth.com.

JUSTINE ELYOT has written extensively for Black Lace and Xcite. She lives in the U.K.

LANA FOX's erotica has been published in anthologies and audio books by Xcite. She also has a story in *Alison's Wonderland*, edited by Alison Tyler. Lana is currently working on an erotic collection and can be found online at lanafox.com.

RACHEL GREEN is a fortysomething writer from Derbyshire, England. She lives with her two partners and three dogs. She was the regional winner of the Undiscovered Authors 2007 and her novel, *An Ungodly Child*, was published in 2008.

SUSIE HARA's work has been published (under her name as well as the pseudonym Lisa Wolfe) in *Best American Erotica 2003*, *Best Women's Erotica 2007*, *Hot Women's Erotica*, *Best of Best Women's Erotica* and *X: The Erotic Treasury*. Writing sexy stories is the most fun she's ever had with a laptop.

LILY HARLEM lives in rural Wales and won the 2009 Love-Honey Vulgari Award for Erotic Fiction. Previously a nurse, she now lets her imagination run wild and free at the keyboard, and her sensual stories can be found in Violet Blue's *Best Women's Erotica 2010* and as e-books on Total-E-Bound.

LOUISA HART's (louisaharte.com) erotic fiction appears in the Cleis Press anthologies *Best Women's Erotica 2010* and *Fairy Tale Lust*. Currently living in New Zealand, she finds inspiration from many places, including her thoughts, dreams and fantasies.

DUSTY HORN's culture writing has been published in McSweeney's *The Believer, Maxmum RnR* and *Kitchen Sink* and read at Perverts Put Out, Femina Potens' Sizzle, and San Francisco's Litquake. Horn pens, publishes and distributes a nominal sex worker memoir/critical theory zine, which was recently featured in Art XX.

NOELLE KEELY is a pseudonym for an extremely prolific erotica writer.

As a coed studying biochemistry and genetics, **LOLITA LOPEZ** (lolitalopez.com) dabbled in creating naughty tales to entertain her friends. Study for a midterm or pen a deliciously dirty story to delight her small band of fans? Not surprisingly, Lo traded science for writing full-time. She lives in Texas with her family.

SYLVIA LOWRY divides her time between Minneapolis and Saint-Germain-des-Prés, Paris. She writes about sex with an enthusiastic fusion of elegance and unbridled explicitness and adores the keen, open exploration of both the literary and the erotic. Her work has appeared in Clean Sheets, The Erotic Woman, Blackheart Magazine, and *Scarlet*.

JADE MELISANDE lives in the Midwest with her two partners and a rescue mutt with social anxiety. She works in nonprofit when she isn't writing erotica, running, traveling or blogging about kinky sex or polyamorous relationships.

VELVET MOORE is a twentysomething who began writing erotica-style works during adolescence and officially entered the world of erotic fiction several years ago. She has been published on the Web at sites including Clean Sheets, the Erotic Woman, and For the Girls. She currently resides in Ohio and makes her living as a corporate writer.

Erotica by **TERESA NOELLE ROBERTS** has appeared in *Bottoms Up, Dirty Girls, Best Women's Erotica 2004, 2006* and *2007*, and many other anthologies with titles that make her mother blush. She also writes erotic romance for Samhain and Phaze.

CHARLOTTE STEIN has published a number of stories in various erotic anthologies, including *Sexy Little Numbers*. Her own collection of short stories is titled *The Things That Make Me Give In*, and her first novella is titled *Waiting In Vain*.

DONNA GEORGE STOREY loves sex and all things Japanese. She is the author of *Amorous Woman*, a very steamy tale of an American woman's love affair with Japan. Her short erotic fiction has been published in numerous anthologies including *Best Women's Erotica, Best American Erotica,* and *Please, Sir.* Read more of her work at DonnaGeorgeStorey.com.

VANESSA VAUGHN's writing has appeared in numerous Cleis Press anthologies, including the *Best Women's Erotica* and *Best Lesbian Erotica* series. She is an author who believes that the best erotica—like the best sex—always includes the unexpected. Learn more about her and her current writing projects at vanessavaughn.com.

KENDRA WAYNE's identity is a poorly kept secret. She has many other publications under many other names, and many other secrets, some of which are harder to entice out of her. She dares you to try.

ABOUT
THE EDITOR

RACHEL KRAMER BUSSEL (rachelkramerbussel.com) is a New York–based author, editor and blogger. She has over thirty books of erotica, including *Fast Girls; Peep Show; Bottoms Up: Spanking Good Stories; Spanked; Naughty Spanking Stories from A to Z 1* and *2; The Mile High Club; Do Not Disturb; Tasting Him; Tasting Her; Please, Sir; Please, Ma'am; He's on Top; She's on Top; Caught Looking; Hide and Seek; Crossdressing; Rubber Sex* and *Bedding Down*. She writes a biweekly sex column for *Sexis* Magzine and is the author of the novel *Everything But...* and the nonfiction book *How to Write an Erotic Love Letter, Best Sex Writing* series editor, and winner of 3 IPPY (Independent Publisher) Awards. Her work has been published in over one hundred anthologies, including *Best American Erotica 2004* and *2006*, Zane's *Chocolate Flava 2* and *Purple Panties, Everything You Know About Sex Is Wrong, Single State of the Union* and *Desire: Women Write About Wanting*. She serves as senior editor at *Penthouse Variations* and wrote the popular "Lusty

Lady" column for the *Village Voice.*

Rachel has written for *AVN, Bust,* Cleansheets.com, *Cosmopolitan, Curve,* the Daily Beast, Fresh Yarn, TheFrisky.com, Gothamist, Huffington Post, Mediabistro, *Newsday, New York Post, Penthouse, Playgirl, Radar, San Francisco Chronicle, Time Out New York* and *Zink,* among others. She has appeared on "The Martha Stewart Show," "The Berman and Berman Show," NY1, and Showtime's "Family Business." She has hosted In the Flesh Erotic Reading Series (inthefleshreadingseries.com) since October 2005, featuring readers from Susie Bright to Zane, about which the *New York Times*'s UrbanEye newsletter said she "welcomes eroticism of all stripes, spots and textures." She blogs at lustylady.blogspot.com.

Printed in the United States
By Bookmasters